ST. JOHN'S LUTHERAN
ELEMENTARY SCHOOL
"...t-Centered Education"
...nda Vista Ave.
...o, Cali...

J
TEA
Teal, Mildred
Bird of passage

DATE DUE

FEB 22			

Books by John and Mildred Teal

PORTRAIT OF AN ISLAND
LIFE AND DEATH OF THE SALT MARSH
THE SARGASSO SEA
PIGEONS AND PEOPLE

Books by Mildred Teal

THE FLIGHT OF THE KITE MERRIWEATHER
BIRD OF PASSAGE

BIRD OF PASSAGE

BIRD OF PASSAGE

Mildred Teal

Illustrated by Ted Lewin

AN ATLANTIC MONTHLY PRESS BOOK
LITTLE, BROWN AND COMPANY—
BOSTON–TORONTO

FIRST EDITION

T04/77

LIBRARY OF CONGRESS CATALOGING IN PUBLICATION DATA

Teal, Mildred.
    Bird of passage.

    "An Atlantic monthly press book."
    SUMMARY: The Great Blue Heron living on the coastal marshes of Georgia and New England becomes a symbol of survival for the characters of two short stories.
    [1. Herons—Fiction. 2. Indians of North America—Fiction. 3. Frontier and pioneer life—Fiction. 4. Lewin, Ted] I. Lewin, Ted. II. Title.
PZ7.T2196Bi   [Fic]   76-54278
ISBN 0-316-83452-1

ATLANTIC–LITTLE, BROWN BOOKS
ARE PUBLISHED BY
LITTLE, BROWN AND COMPANY
IN ASSOCIATION WITH
THE ATLANTIC MONTHLY PRESS

*Published simultaneously in Canada
by Little, Brown & Company (Canada) Limited*

PRINTED IN THE UNITED STATES OF AMERICA

To
Nina Jessie Hightower Mann

Part One

1

A young blue heron stood in lone dignity on the Gloucester marsh. When he fed, his stiltlike legs carried him along with careful majesty. The slow gait was ill-suited for hunting meadow mice and shrews but each step carried him nearer the small furred creatures that ran for life.

The big bird hunted the fresh ponds carved out of the granite shoreline and the salt pools left by ebbing tides on the marshes. He grew fat on minnows and small fish that darted like silver arrows from the deadly thrusts of his strong bill. Paths through the grasses marked his pursuit of young black snakes.

On the edge of the upland earlier that spring the young heron had caught frogs as they hopped their way from moist woodlands to the freshwater pools, attracted there by the buzzing din of hundreds of other frogs advertising for mates.

Then late one summer morning, when steam rose toward the hot sun after a cool night, he was joined by an old heron who settled down to fish the same creeks and stalk the same marsh meadows.

The old bird's large body had once been strong and sleek. Now the rufous feathers at the top of his legs were scruffy and the long black feathers on his white crown jutted raggedly from his head. The color of his bill was a faded yellow, but time had left his hearing acute and his light eyes still sharp enough to see to a far horizon.

Wisdom and wariness kept him safe. He was king of the marsh, bigger than most creatures that moved over its wet surface.

Now he was a fugitive. He had been driven from the nest he shared with his mate in a heronry of ten breeding pairs. The nest was an old one, three feet deep and four feet wide. It had been carelessly constructed of loosely woven, coarse sticks and contained holes so large the first eggs were in danger of falling to the ground. Anchored haphazardly in the joint of two branches high in the top of a large spruce tree, nest and birds survived the year.

Each year thereafter the old heron and his mate had lined the nest with ever smaller twigs. Finally it became cemented tight with the white guano put out by each year's chicks as they inexpertly tried to defecate over its edge. The squawking put up by the baby birds, and the clambering through the branches as the parents flew near, would have attracted humans if the heronry were not built inaccessibly deep in the forest.

Several days ago his mate had flown off to feed. She did not return. While he himself was feeding the nest was taken by a young pair of herons. The monarch had fought but he was no match for the young, vigorous birds. He flew off to roost nearby, staying on the fringes of the heronry. Then he left and had come to roost on a small tree near the marsh where the young great blue heron fished.

The young bird with sleek plumage and the wise old heron fell to taking turns at sentinel duty. While one stalked the marsh, probing the tall streamside grasses for bittern eggs and the shorter grasses on high marsh for young meadowlarks, the other stood nearby, ready to give

[4]

out a honking distress call if danger appeared. The humans that invaded the Gloucester marshes were usually busy with their own pursuits, clamming or hay gathering, but the wary birds still took to the air if they drew too close. Their flight alerted hundreds of other birds living and nesting near the marsh. Soon the air would be filled with gulls, terns, larks, and redwings. When all danger had passed, the herons would return to their place of feeding.

Summer neared its end. As the days shortened the two herons stood motionless for long periods, their large bodies reflected in the rippling water. They fished less actively now, eating just enough to maintain the cushion of fat that would sustain them on their long flight. The young bird had already spent two winters on an island off the coast of Georgia. Once again he would set out when the combination of short and cool days on the northern marsh signaled that the time was right. On this passage he would have the old bird's company.

Still they waited, affected neither by the tides nor by the doings of humans. Days dawned and died. The pattern of the birds' lives followed passageways established so long ago that their beginnings were lost in the dimness of time.

2

Far to the south, in the foothills of the Appalachian mountains, another passage began. A boy and his mother stole like thieves from their own house during the darkest hour of the darkest moon.

They had discarded white man's clothes and put on high-topped walking moccasins and buckskin clothing. Each carried two skin bags covered with oiled cloth. Divided between the bags were food for several days and extra clothing. Across his chest, the boy wore his hunting bow. Hanging from his belt was a knife and a quiver of sharp, true arrows. His mother carried her skinning knife and a hatchet. The gun they had left behind, for they had to travel light and fast.

Inside the house burned a small wick set to start a blaze that would first flame weakly then devour everything they left behind.

Thin, restless breezes rattled oak leaves. A soft thud came from the corral as the pony ridded himself of a biting fly. The boy slipped away to open the corral gate so the pony could wander away. The pigs they had slaughtered earlier in the evening and left strewn about the barnyard as if cut down by raiders. The cattle they had driven out to fend for themselves in the brush. At the first hint of dawn, the pony, the boy's pride and love, trained to turn and run with only the slightest pressure on his bare flanks, would leave the corral to go to the water. The pony might be killed by raiders, or stolen, but the little brown mare still had a wild edge and she might take to the brush to scatter with the cattle.

A pall of smoke from gutted houses hung on the air. The fetid odor of seared flesh stung the boy's nostrils as he moved toward his waiting mother.

Together they slipped away, the boy nearly as tall as the woman but with the disjointed movement of recent growth. They moved silently through the black night past the cooling ashes of his grandmother's and his father's sister's house.

The boy saw in his mind the bright light of day made brighter by flames that reached from his aunt's house into the sky. The two horses and cows lay slain and his own father lay with outstretched arms and a wild and horrible grimace. Beneath his gaping face, three musket balls had torn through his chest.

The boy heard again the thundering hooves of fast horses, saw the masked faces of daytime raiders who swept through the farm clearing. As was the custom, the boy's father had gone ahead to see to his sister's children. The boy and his mother followed close enough to become horrified witnesses to his death.

They had been hidden by a thicket of willows that sprang along the banks of the Ocmulgee. His mother, her black eyes wild, fear and anger creasing her flat face, started forward. The movement was cumbersome for she was large with the baby inside her. Before she was free of the thicket she knew that her help would be futile. She quietly shrank back toward the boy. The raiders wore red cloths over their faces but there was no doubt they were white men.

The first white invaders into the Creek territory had been welcomed, the next tolerated with unease, and the last, a new breed bent on driving the Creeks from their ancient lands, were feared. The Creek had been the most civilized of people, taking the ways, dress, and farming techniques of the white man. They intermarried. Some owned slaves and ran prosperous farms. Their lands had been assured them for eternity by the federal government in Washington, D.C.

There were many Indians, sensing the inevitability of destruction, who moved ahead of the raiders to the west where the federal government had set aside large tracts of land bought from Napoleon. The western lands were poor, not fertile like their foothills. The way of life the Creeks had borrowed from the white man was swept away in the move westward. They lived from day to day, from hand to mouth, like their forefathers. Many who chose the path to the west found it marked with the fresh, shallow graves of other Indians.

Now the boy and his mother moved silently toward the river. The faintest rim of light appeared on the horizon. There could be only an hour of travel before daylight. Then they would have to hide. Even with so little time, the woman turned down a hidden pathway to where her mother lay on a pallet of skins under a natural bower of overhanging trees. She was old, her hair completely white and wispy, her face a map of wrinkles, her body twisted by the weight of years. She could not make the trek with them. Neither could she stay.

The faintest noise came from the bower. Soon his mother moved toward the boy again, her shoulders hunkered.

She stopped for a short time and did not move. An unsung death wail hung on the air and the boy knew his grandmother was dead. There was no time to scratch even a shallow grave. They must leave both husband and the old one to be picked clean by carrion eaters, their bones scattered. They would not be picked by the tribal bone picker and bundled in a burial packet.

The boy felt the weight of his mother's sorrow, and he felt fear. Would they die? Would their bones be scattered by wild animals? His cheeks were still round with youth but he was already at the age when he should have joined a war party and been scratched by the Mico. It was time to

[8]

drop his baby name like a used garment and to gain a new name.

He would have been scratched but there was dissension among the elders, the Micos. Some said they would get along with the white man, for hadn't the two nations been friends for a hundred years? Others said, "What land we have left is but large enough to live and walk on." With the Micos in disorder, the old customs died. The war parties no longer rode forth and the young boys did not have a chance to prove themselves. Now each man and family was bent toward survival.

A freshet breeze stirred the woman into action. With a shudder and shake of her head she put aside thoughts of her mother, her dead husband, and her home, and without a backward glance she turned her face to the southeast.

The boy knew only vaguely where they were going. Tales had been told to him of the place. Songs of their home on the Georgia mainland and the coastal islands had been handed down through his mother's family for a hundred years. Their people had been reduced to a pitiful remnant by war and disease and had slipped westward to join the Creeks in the low foothills of the Georgia mountains. They had settled down, intermarried, and eventually melted into the farming life of the white man.

The boy and woman would go back to the coast to one specific island, Sapelo, that lay many days' travel to the southeast. They would go on foot, traveling by night, resting by day, following the river that started first as a tumbling mountain stream then broadened into a muddy delta as other streams joined it near the coast. They would eat what they could carry or gather, not daring a fire to betray their camp. They must play the game of the hunted, always running ahead of the hunter. To stay meant a sure and painful death; to move westward also meant death, no less painful because it came on the dull slow feet of hunger or disease. The boy and his mother turned their faces to the southeast.

3

Even though the days were warm the predawn air carried a thin edge of winter. The last full autumn moon had shrunk to a crescent. The Indians' journey should not take more than from the crescent to the next full moon but the woman moved clumsily with her unborn child. The woman and boy trod the last hour before this dawn on muted feet.

At one time they heard a hound coming swiftly toward them from a distance, excited and on a trail. Quickly they immersed themselves in the river under overhanging branches. They held their packs and weapons overhead to keep them dry. The dog veered off and from the pattern of high-pitched barks they knew he had treed a wild animal — that he was after different game.

As the sun broke over the rim of earth, they sought shelter. The territory was still familiar but they had moved out of the realm of neighbors onto the ground of strangers. The greatest danger would come from chance encounter. Each white man owned at least one gun and wouldn't hesitate to use it, even against an unarmed Indian woman and a boy not yet scratched.

The sun breaking over the rim of earth would shine on the raiders. They would stir in their campsites and prepare for their day's work. Among the Creeks there had been talk that the raiders were paid by the federal government. The State of Georgia had made an agreement with the federal government. Georgia would give up all claim to a region to the west if Georgia lands were rid of the Indian Nations. But who could know if this was true?

Who, too, could know if the Micos took for themselves tributes from the federal government, even those marked for the whole of the Creek Nation. Some said the chiefs grew fat on the leanness of their own people.

As the sun came up, the boy found grim satisfaction thinking of the raiders who killed his father. They would come to his father's farm to find the squash and pumpkins smashed in the fields, the cornstalks broken, and the ears scattered for raccoons and crows. Ruin would meet the raiders and rob them of their mad greed. Faces had been covered but the boy remembered the hard glitter of the raiders' eyes as they rode toward his father. Defenseless, he had stood for what seemed an eternity before he gave a war cry and unarmed had rushed toward them.

For their rest the mother and son had chosen a copse of trees which grew thickly enough to shelter them from view in every direction. They were close enough to water so that the two could slip in to confuse dogs if, by chance, they picked up the trail.

The mother took a piece of dried pressed meat and berries from her pack. She broke off a chunk and passed it to the boy. The boy dug in his pack for two pieces of hard baked cornmeal. They dipped water from the clear running river and wetted the cornmeal in their mouths.

From the protective canopy of the copse they saw three deer treading along a well-worn path to the riverside. Two does were followed by an immature male from this year's birth, his spots a ghostly shadow of his fawn's coat.

Toward afternoon, when the heat rose from the warmed earth, the boy and his mother smelled the smoke from a distant fire. Neither spoke but each felt the stab of sorrow and pain carried through the air.

They dozed and slept and woke time after time. Flies found them and disturbed their sleep. Toward evening the deer returned, again treading the same path. The Indians attended to their needs, and as the sun dropped below the horizon, they set out swiftly. The chance meeting with raiders lessened with each passing minute, for white men liked to sit, smoke, and belch over their evening meal.

The boy and woman ran beside the river while they could still see, covering in one hour a distance that it would take them the rest of the night to duplicate. Their high-topped moccasins snagged on brush but they dared not tread a more used path. Several times the boy had to slow down while his mother caught up.

Suddenly, as the last glow of twilight dimmed, the woman tripped on a root. The boy saw her clutch her swollen belly. With a hissing intake of breath she fell heavily and lay stunned. The boy knelt beside her in fear. She pushed his hand from her shoulder, slowly got up and walked on doggedly.

4

Dawn found the Indians in unfamiliar territory. Already they were well down the foothills where other streams flowed into the river. They crossed the widening water by pushing logs before them to which they had lashed their packs.

The night's exertion had cost the woman dearly. Beads of perspiration swelled over her upper lip and shone on her forehead. Her dark eyes were dull with pain as she sank under a bush.

The boy saw her condition but urged her on still farther, to a denser thicket. In the distance a white man's house reflected the sun. It must be part of a plantation. The slaves' houses would probably be near the river, some distance from the big house. Black men would be walking to the fields to begin the day's work. They would be singing or talking as they walked and the Indians would have warning of their coming.

The boy did hear singing, not the chanting song of his tribe, but a throaty and rhythmic rumble. The song hung on the air and grew faint. The men were moving away from them.

The warming sun lulled the boy to sleep. Suddenly he awoke with an inward start. The air hung heavy with panting. A fly settled on his face. It was not that which had awakened him. All his life flies had settled on his face. Then he heard a small scratching. Alert now, the boy strained his ears to hear and his eyes to see. His mother was gone. The panting continued. He knew. Drops of blood, brightly red, led to the densest part of the thicket.

Hastily the boy scattered dirt on the fresh blood. It would draw scavengers. He drew aside a branch covering the entrance to a small clearing and saw his mother squatting, working in the dirt before her. For a brief moment he glimpsed a small and motionless form in the depression.

His mother turned with panic in her eyes, saw the boy, and violently gestured him away. He turned and moved silently back to his sleeping place. He could do nothing but wait. He had seen what he should not have seen.

Soon his mother came back and fell heavily to the ground. The boy started toward the hollowed-out spot, but again his mother motioned him away with a gesture that told him everything had been taken care of. In the face of such new, awesome happenings he felt helpless.

He did risk going to the river over open ground to get water in one of the skin bags. He bathed his mother's face and then let her wash herself. He carefully carried the dirty water back to the river so it would wash downstream and not leave a scent. The woman fell into a deep, exhausted sleep. She moaned; twice she ground her teeth with a loud rasping noise.

The sun set on the second day but the boy and his mother didn't move from the shelter. She was weak and he felt the fever in her body. He fed her from his hand. Again and again he bathed her. Each time he went to the water he risked exposure, but go he must for this was the only way he knew to care for her. Toward the third morning she broke into a heavy sweat and slept through that day and the night.

When a distant cock's crow floated clearly on the predawn air, the boy woke his mother. He gave her some pressed berries and hard cornmeal, today his portion as well as hers. Hardly had she finished when he urged her out into the open. They would have to move, even if a short distance, for the dead child would soon attract the earth diggers. They had already been too long in one spot.

The Indians waded close to shore, pulling themselves along on overhanging branches that dipped toward the water. They moved as fast as the woman could until they reached an open spot in the river. There was no protection.

With as little motion as possible they melted against the bank and onto the land.

Again the boy gave his portion of food to his mother, this time keeping a bit for himself. She accepted without emotion or thanks. To reach the island that lay at the journey's end, they would need each other.

That day passed, and the next, the mother growing in strength. The boy was on short rations. Each mile passed torturously underfoot until the moon set. They stopped and slept during the daylight hours. The sun rose and set and again the two moved as swiftly as they could.

During the journey the landscape gradually changed. Trees grew closer together along the river which now turned and snaked through gentle foothills. More and more of the rolling hills were cleared and planted. Abruptly they reached the fall line which truly separated mountain from plain.

5

Each day's sun found the two great blue herons stalking meadow mice or fishing. The wary old heron and the young, strong bird waited for a cold front to pass to the southeast. All around them on the Gloucester marsh and inland, hundreds of thousands of birds were feeding and resting. The young birds flew to teach their muscles the strength needed to carry them southward. Tens of thousands of adult birds had flown on earlier southeast winds out over the Atlantic Ocean, following the shortest route to winter feeding grounds in South America.

The herons would take another flight path, directly south and down the coast, at a right angle to the Indian boy and his mother who moved toward the east and daylight.

Perspiration ran down the woman's face. She held her side with one hand. The boy knew she couldn't go on at the pace he had set. Only a few minutes remained before dawn and light glowed on the woman's glistening face.

Suddenly they rounded a bend in the river and nearly blundered into a small dugout canoe tied to a crude log ramp. Far up a clearing the boy saw a lean-to such as trappers build for a temporary shelter. Smoke came from a hidden fire.

The boy motioned his mother to move downstream. She passed the boat and ramp safely. Not a sound came from the lean-to. The morning air hung heavy. The boy silently waded to the canoe and looked inside. In the bottom lay a bundle of skins. One paddle lay across a rawhide seat, another was lashed under the seat. A long pole stretched the length of the canoe. The boy took his knife from the top of his moccasin, where he wore it white-man style. He cut through the tie rope. Suddenly he felt a rush and heard a roar as a creature burst from the bushes beside him.

For a blind moment the boy thought it was a bear. It wore white man's clothes and a dense beard covered the face. Beetling brows, so thick they seemed to join in the middle, reached almost to the man's hairline. Hair sprouted from his nostrils and ears. With another roar the man clutched the boy's throat with massive hands.

In blind panic the boy drove the knife, still clasped in his hand, deep into the man's upper arm. The hairy one, more monster than man, seemed not to notice. The boy was choked and shaken until his senses fled. Waves of blood red exploded behind his eyes. Then waves of darkness washed the red away. The boy forced himself to open his eyes and with one desperate thrust drove his knife upward. It sank deep under the man's ribs and tore upward. A final black wave washed the boy into unconsciousness.

When he swam back to awareness, he felt the movement of the river. He sensed that he was in the canoe. He opened his eyes to see his mother standing in the bow, frantically poling along the river's bank. The boy's throat burned with liquid fire. His tongue felt swollen. The bulk of a man floated astern, face down, arms outstretched as he had fallen. The boy welcomed the blackness that washed over him again.

He awoke only after the woman had tied the canoe in a hidden spot. The woman lay beside him and they both slept through the day. At sunset they pushed the canoe into midstream. They traveled fast, the dugout slipping through the water like a fish.

The boy felt sick. The dead man and the crimson stain on the boy's knife were left behind but he could not wash the vision from behind his eyelids. Still he took his turn in the poling position while his mother rested in the bottom of the canoe.

Morning brought them to one of the many forks along the river. They turned upstream. They knew the river here would narrow down into a passage overhung and protected. The river twisted into a swamp almost as dark as the night they were just leaving. Great looping vines swung from trees that rose like solemn giants from murky black water. Cypress roots broke the water like so many thick, knotted fingers reaching upward. Festoons of gray-green Spanish moss hung from the tree branches and muted the sound of waking birds.

Here in the swamp, for the first time since the day raiders swept over the Creek lands, the woman and boy felt safe. White men seldom entered these treacherous river swamps. When they did they were helpless as children.

The boy tied the dugout to a tree even though there was little motion to the water and they both lay down to sleep. At midday they awoke and ate. Here they could risk talking. Their voices fell strangely on their ears, for they had neither spoken nor heard speech for many days and nights.

The mother began hesitantly. "I have wondered if it would be proper for me to do this. There is no one to tell me yes or no, so I follow my own counsel.

"It is time to give you your new name." She took the skinning knife from her belt. "You fought bravely in battle and truly you have earned it.

"I don't know the proper words that the Mico would say, but I make my own small ceremony." She whetted the knife on her moccasin. "I call on these trees to witness. From now on you will be called 'Juanillo' after the great Mico who long ago protected the islands we are going to. He was strong. You are strong and you will be strong. He was brave. You will be brave like him and your father. Your wisdom will be that of the most ancient of Micos."

With each statement she made a scratch on the boy's arm with the point of the knife.

"Your baby name is lost forever in the waters of this swamp." She dipped the knife blade in the water.

Juanillo's last baby act was to feel his eyes smart. This was the sought-after manhood? The thing he and his companions had longed for, bragged about, and fought over? His rise to manhood was to witness his father's death, was

to see his grandmother dead and left unburied, his brother or sister, he knew not which, lying stillborn in a grave forgotten, and the final act, the killing of a man by his own hand.

Behind the words "manhood" and "bravery" lay deep feelings — fear, rage, and even compassion, for hadn't he tasted and felt blind fear when he thought he would die from the man's hands around his throat? Hadn't he raged against his father's murderers, and hadn't he cried silently for his mother when she buried the wizened child?

Now he was named Juanillo and he must take on the role of strong protector along with the name. It was with some doubt that he said; "I will act as a man. Juanillo will be my guide, but you must teach me as my father would, since he isn't here."

The ceremony was over. They were again mother and son fleeing for their lives.

For the rest of the day they breathed freely, slept, talked and ate sparingly. The small store of food was giving out. The boy had a few corn cakes left in his bag and his mother but a little dried meat and berries. From now on the land would have to support them. Juanillo tried catching the fish that moved sluggishly through the murky swamp water. Each time he thought he had one, it slipped through his hands. From now on their greatest danger would not be so much from discovery or pursuit but from lack of food. The cool of the evenings would sap their strength but the bundle of skins in the bottom of the canoe would help them meet even the rigors of winter.

Well before sunset they untied the canoe and poled their way out of the swamp. It was already dark with shadows. Soon they would not be able to follow the twisting creek. They paddled out into wide water and made many miles before twilight deepened into night.

6

◇◇◇◇◇

They were aided in the night's travel by the moon, rising nearly full and lighting the water with mellow warmth. Wedges of honking geese flew south, silhouetted against the moon's face. They flew strongly and a shorter distance than the herons would travel.

Juanillo and his mother traveled beneath, but to the east. Juanillo wondered as he looked at the geese. He saw the leader of a wedge drop back and another take his place. "Why shouldn't the leader always lead?" He put this in the back of his mind to think on later.

The river passed swiftly under the canoe. There was danger in every log floating in the water. The dugout was sturdy, but the boy and woman could be thrown into the water if it struck one of these half-submerged logs.

Plantation clearings opened up here and there, but for the most part the buildings and the big houses were away from the water, away from the hovering swamp miasma which bred a deadly fever that killed people of all races.

Toward morning his mother paddled vigorously for the river bank. Juanillo did not know why she did so but he followed her lead and paddled hard. Then into the boy's consciousness came the noise of a great number of small birds.

Juanillo, bent on his own thoughts, had been unaware of the fluttering and twitter of the hundreds of birds. This was no way for a man to behave. He must be as alert as his mother from now on and stop dreaming. He felt shame and his baby name flashed into his mind.

A flock of small birds gathered on a large patch of grass planted in shallow water. The canoe caught in the muddy bottom, then freed itself as a small drainage canal opened just wide enough to permit the passage of the dugout.

Many of the small birds flew into the air and noisily retreated out of sight. Others paid little attention to the boy and his mother but kept feeding on the grain heads hanging near the water's surface. Rice! The patch looked abandoned and had gone wild, but it still produced. The mother grabbed handfuls of the reedy grass, bent them over the side of the canoe and beat the grain heads into the bottom with her paddle. They quickly scooped as much as they could into the empty skin bags.

Suddenly all the birds took flight and Juanillo and his mother stopped dead. The dull fear that had ridden with them since they left their farm suddenly sharpened. Juanillo felt a sickness rising in his stomach. Were they once more the quarry? His mother cautiously turned her head to listen in all directions. Whatever put the birds to flight seemed to hold no danger for the Indians, but they paddled away stealthily. The dread of a surprise attack gnawed at them.

There was no safe place to stop for the day. The river broadened. Many tributaries cut into it in a maze of creeks and waterways. Half the day was spent following a false stream that looked like the river but which led them into another swamp. They backtracked through its confused twistings and turnings.

[21]

They had paddled for many hours, all night and most of the day. Now they would have to rest. Letting the current carry them on they ate the last of their meat and corn cakes. The mother husked some of the rice and put it to soak in a large leaf she had plucked from a tree.

For the remainder of the day they sheltered under a canopy of trees. The canoe floated among reeds and strange plants that grew from the bottom. A peace that comes from the removal of physical danger felt too long settled over the woman and boy. It seemed they had existed always in this world of water and animals and plants. Frogs jumped into the water. A few sluggish snakes hung from low tree branches.

The horror of their voyage receded with each day's passage. Their minds could absorb no more pain and sorrow and blocked out all thoughts of home for a time. They would grieve, but grieving would steal upon them unaware on a remembered odor or a half-remembered shadow caught in the corner of an eye.

Streams entered the mother river everywhere along the way. The canoe was carried ever faster toward the sea. There was no turning back. For their meal they risked a small fire in the bottom of the canoe. The mother heated the water-swollen rice. Juanillo finally succeeded in catching a fish with his bare hands. No danger lay in the fire itself, for the boat had been hollowed by burning and scraping. When they had finished they threw embers from the smoldering boat into the water, and scraped clean the blackened hot area.

After the meal, bigger than those they were now used to, they fell into a stuporous sleep. While they slept the wind changed. It blew strongly and bitingly toward the southeast and woke the Indians.

The canoe moved jerkily, catching frequently when it was drawn too near shore. Juanillo and his mother had to paddle to stay in midstream. Strange new odors borne on the cold front assailed their nostrils, vegetable odors mixed with decay and salt. Here and there stands of tall, sharply spiked grass grew down to the water's edge. As they paddled Juanillo could see schools of small, silver-sided fish scurrying away from the paddle blade. Crabs slipped sideways into the water and swam downward toward the soft ooze of the bottom.

"We have one more day's travel," his mother said. "We will have to keep alert for signs of white men. The island is said to be uninhabited but who knows how many other people have the same idea we have? I am not a tracker. Right now we could use your father's guidance for he could track far better than I. Your father knew which way the bear turned to face the sun, and where the turkeys gathered to fan their tails. And he knew what path white man and Indian had passed along. You must remember everything he told you about the ways of animals and men for I have been too long tending the garden.

"For now, I know we must keep the banks of the land on our left side, and look through every opening in the water to the right. Sapelo will lie on the horizon about the distance we can see. When we find the waterway to the island we will have to strike out for there will be no shelter. From then on we must paddle hard."

They lay down to rest and gather strength for the last push. All around them rose vast meadows of tall grass like no others they had ever seen. They seemed to stretch mile after mile. Some of the grassy salt marshes were awash with tide water, others high and dry.

Juanillo was first to see the island as the canoe nosed out

[23]

from behind an especially verdant marsh. Sapelo lay to the east, hours away, its long, low, hazy profile slumbering on the horizon.

Mother and son stopped paddling for an excited moment, then bent to their task.

7

The first chill gusts of the cold front blew across the Gloucester marsh. As the temperature dropped and the winds increased, ripples played over the surface of the creeks and ponds. The wind picked up intensity and the ripples grew to small waves. A salty froth collected around the pond's edges. During the late afternoon the tide rose higher than usual, covering even the highest portions of the marsh. The two herons huddled a distance apart. Occasionally they shifted position and stretched their necks and wings.

Following some secret signal the young great blue heron thrust his head forward, took a few steps, and with long, powerful wing beats mounted into the air. Within seconds the old bird followed. Both rose higher, striking out southward, their long necks tucked back between their wings, their legs outstretched behind them.

As they passed over the upland bordering the marsh, there was an unexpected movement below. The old bird struggled to fly higher.

There was a burst of musket fire, followed by the noise of the percussion. An acrid smell of burning gunpowder blew upward.

The musket ball tore through the old bird's wing. Wind whistled through his feathers as he plummeted earthward frantically beating the air with his one good wing. He continued falling, caught in death.

The young bird had felt a sudden blow on his bill. The musket ball slowed and veered slightly after it hit the old bird's wing. Otherwise it would have torn away the young bird's bill. Blood rushed to the wound, but in panic the bird flew on.

Throughout the night he steadily winged his way over the coastal towns of New England. The landscape was dark except for an occasional glow from cottage windows.

On he flew over Long Island Sound, crossing the salt meadows along the island's southern shore, and over the sea again, still riding the southeast winds of the cold front. Flying close to the water, the heron winged down the New Jersey coast as Juanillo and his mother began their last day's paddle toward Sapelo.

The strong winds continued eastward but the great blue heron broke his flight over the ocean and came back toward land at Kittyhawk, North Carolina. Barrier islands, sounds, marshes, and coastal plains, bathed in the quickening light of day, passed beneath him.

Warmth flowed from the earth. The winds diminished. The threat of northern winter lay far behind him. Ducks dabbled in ponds below and a wedge of Canada geese flew high on the horizon.

The two Indians dipped their paddles in the waterway between long reaches of salt marsh. Their arms throbbed from continuous paddling.

[25]

Juanillo looked to his right. "We are here!" he said.

His mother glanced up. "This is an island, but not Sapelo. Sapelo must have tall trees as well as scrub and it must still be farther away. This is a hummock. Not fit for living on."

Juanillo's cheeks burned. He was wrong. He must learn not to let childish eagerness cloud his judgment.

"Never mind," his mother said. "The island will come soon enough now. We must save our strength for the swift current."

The great blue heron flew lower. His wings no longer beat powerfully. His reserve of energy ran low. Now the territory took on the familiarity of his winter feeding ground. Here food grew abundantly and snows fell only once in a human generation. Like a specter he sailed over the rivers and creeks and vast marshlands that stretched in a broad belt along the coast.

An imperceptible rise of water carried Juanillo and his mother up and out of the trough of creeks lined with the exposed roots of a forest of tall marsh grass. The two Indians could now see to all sides. The tide flowed strongly beneath the dugout as they paddled through a sea of inter-mixed grass and water. Hummocks of taller grass rose here and there. Some hummocks even sported twisted, scrubby, wind-pruned trees. In other areas, short, sparse grass seemed to grow right out of the water. Now Sapelo lay close by. There could be no mistake. It rested like a drowsing giant gently buoyed on the rising tide.

An awesome stretch of open water must be crossed to reach their goal. Six strong men would have been a better match for it than a young man newly named and his weak-ened mother.

[26]

The great blue heron steadily lost altitude. He had flown from yesterday's dusk to this day's afternoon. The long pull on the wing muscles strained his breast and his whole body. He needed rest and food but he had not yet reached the spot he looked for. He flew on.

In the middle of the sound Juanillo rested for a short time with the paddle across his knees, mindful that his mother's strength was fading. "Are you ready?" he asked, trying to encourage her. There was nothing to do but cross this last stretch. He knew they must risk all to gain the hoped-for shelter.

His mother grunted, saving even the small energy she would expend on an answer. For two hours they battled relentless currents that tore at the canoe and threatened to carry them up a broader river to a spot distant from their goal.

As their strength failed, the miracle of the turning tide carried them across open water and allowed them to head up a narrow river that coursed by the island. So exhausted were they that they did not recognize the part the tide played in their journey.

The two Indians continued upriver looking for a safe landing. The south end of the island was awash. As they paddled farther, the river narrowed before a bluff. Massive trees grew horizontal branches as large as lesser tree trunks and reaching to the water's edge. A dense growth of Spanish moss hung almost to the ground, shrouding the trees. Juanillo and his mother bent over their paddles, putting forth their last energy. Eyes dull with pain, muscles cramped and aching, they pushed toward the bluff.

The great blue heron flew lower and lower, coasting in at an oblique angle to the river up which Juanillo and his mother paddled. The boy looked up, his face framed by

[27]

long, unkempt cords of black hair, as he felt the rush of air from the great bird's wings.

For a long moment the heron hung in the air over the boy's head, then with startled wing beats rose again to sail farther on and settle by the riverside. Juanillo stopped paddling, in awe of the bird. His mother continued stroking with her paddle. The nose of the canoe touched Sapelo just as the bird folded his wings and stood like a benevolent monarch, graciously allowing the intruders to land on his island.

8

Suddenly Juanillo came to himself and again his cheeks burned. His mother had finished the paddling while he watched the heron. But now he stood erect and caught an overhanging branch so he could steady the canoe as his mother climbed out.

They struggled the canoe onto the bank and fell exhausted under the protective arms of a giant oak. After catching their breath they unloaded the dugout and made it secure. Then, utterly spent, they slept with their heads on the bundle of skins while the sun arched across the heavens.

The great blue heron fed for a time on the schools of silver-sided mummichogs and top minnows that swam near the surface of the river. Then he flew to his rest in a tree on an interior pond on the island. Other birds, smaller white herons and black anhingas, squawked and resettled themselves as the great blue heron flew into the heronry. The pond, though broad, was nearly dark with the overgrowth of trees draped with Spanish moss. Duckweed covered the surface so profusely that little open water remained to reflect the dark shadow of the large bird.

The moon, which had been a ghostly presence in the day sky, brightened and asserted its dominion over the stars. A cool breeze stirred the moss over the boy and his mother. The earth smelled of growing mixed with the musk of decaying plants. They slept.

Juanillo awoke before dawn to the sound of small scratching noises. An animal scuffled through fallen oak leaves in search for acorns. The boy lay quietly, opening his eyes a narrow slit. By the light of the waning moon he silently watched a small mouse with long hind legs jumping from spot to spot. With every stop the mouse rummaged about with his front feet, then abandoned the spot and hopped to another.

A whir of feathered wings, more felt than heard, surrounded Juanillo as a large shadowed owl swooped on the mouse. The owl's large eyes glowed in the moonlight. The mouse jumped in panic for cover but the owl was on it, his wings beating the ground as he hopped after the scuttling prey. Its high-pitched squeaks were suddenly stilled and the owl, with the mouse securely in his grasp, flew away as silently as he had swooped.

From the creek, Juanillo heard the small hissings of bivalves as they opened and closed their shells. Far down the river a large dolphin lolled in the water, swimming and blowing. Juanillo listened to the noises with wonder he had never felt before. He even heard the gentle ripple of waves as they washed along the banks of the river.

Juanillo had long been used to the woods and freshwater

lakes near his farm, but much of the time he had worked the fields with his mother and ridden his pony along mountain pathways, unmindful of the sounds and smells of his familiar homeland. Here, on this island, a new awareness of the earth and sky crept into his consciousness. Sounds and smells and colors, pale in the moonlight, covered him like a blanket. He no longer wandered among trees in an unnoticed landscape. He became brother to all animals who crept and crawled and flew. The island held no terror for him. Sleep took Juanillo gently.

"We must look around before the sun is high." His mother's voice woke him. "There might be others here. I saw a white man's house. It looked abandoned, but we must be sure."

Juanillo rubbed sleep from his eyes and sat up, instantly awake. His mother had been as exhausted as he when they paddled up river, but it was she who had seen the house. Juanillo had seen only the river, the great blue heron, and welcoming trees. A house could mean danger. The fears he felt while on the journey returned in a rush. Hidden, unformed imaginings slipped into his mind and drove out the secure feeling of the night.

"Here, take this! Eat!" His mother gave him a cold lump of rice which he chewed thoughtfully.

"What if men do live here? What if there are others like us here?"

"What if the sun falls from the sky?" his mother answered. "First we will see. Then we will worry."

They set off southward, the mother carrying her skinning knife, Juanillo his bow slung over his shoulder. He looked for the great blue heron, but the bird did not appear.

They walked easily over the open forest floor. A mat of leaves, sifting from live oak trees, covered the ground.

Here and there mother and son crossed well-worn animal pathways. Raccoons, opossums, and deer aplenty lived on the island. Juanillo read the signs in their droppings. Here the deer were small, a poor comparison to the large bucks that roamed the mountains in Creek Indian lands.

They moved along silently, straining to hear sounds of danger. Moving quietly they crossed open areas as quickly as possible. Finally, they picked up a wagon trail winding through a thicket of palmetto. The trail, a faint remnant of old wheel ruts, widened into a roadway between low holly shrubs. When the road branched off onto a larger road mother and son left it and found themselves moving back toward the river they had paddled.

"It must lead to the big house I saw. We should be very careful now." His mother barely breathed.

The morning air magnified sounds from all sides. The distant call of birds floated clearly toward them. It was not for these that they strained, but for voices, coughing, singing, the creak of wheels, the chopping of wood. They crept on through undergrowth and behind tall pine trees that replaced the hollies.

In a clearing ahead they saw a large house made of tabby. To one side lay a row of low buildings. Leading to the big house was a double row of pecan trees with round balls of mistletoe growing among the upper branches. Silence lay over the grounds.

Smoke should be coming from the chimneys if the house was inhabited, for it was white man's breakfast time. That meant a fire in the hearth. People should be coming and going from the low buildings, for they were the slave quarters. Nothing stirred except for birds, gray squirrels, and lizards crawling up the walls.

An air of neglect hung over the settlement and signs of

deterioration had set in. Rotten spots showed in the thatch on the low buildings. Part of a fireplace chimney had crumbled. Portions of the tabby had disintegrated, revealing a large number of oyster shells bound in a mortar of lime and sand.

"It seems empty, but take care!" his mother warned. "We won't go into the house."

They drank deeply from a clear well to one side of the main house. Juanillo picked up as many pecans as he could carry in his buckskin shirt and filled the bottom of his quiver. His mother filled the skin bag she had slung over her shoulder. Juanillo squatted on his haunches while he opened a pecan. The meat was sweet on his tongue.

"If people come to the island they will come here first," said Juanillo's mother and signaled anxiously for them to continue. They backtracked to the north-south roadway and turned southward. They found no footprints. Now they traveled in the roadway but still with caution. Where they were forced to walk entirely without cover, they carefully erased their own moccasin prints with a leafy branch.

The sun was high now. They pressed southward to the very tip of the island. Here they got their first land view of the broad marsh that covered the southern end of Sapelo, the same marsh they had seen as they paddled upriver to their campsite. Tall green grasses rippled like a wheat field in the fall breeze. Everywhere between portions of marsh grew shorter grasses, black rush, and salicornia, Spanish bayonette grew in clumps here and there, the wicked, sharp points of leaves as deadly as they looked.

From everywhere came the sucking noise of water pushing and pulling at the muddy banks of the streamsides, drawing nourishment from the marsh as an infant takes milk from its mother.

Juanillo saw the great blue heron standing in a low creek. There could be no doubt it was the same bird, for his crooked bill set him apart from all others. Again the boy felt that they were on the island with the bird's permission. They would share in its bounty but at any time the monarch might take away the privilege of living and eating from his domain. For as long as the Indians looked over the marsh, the bird stood motionless in the water. Juanillo turned reluctantly to follow his mother when she moved on.

They walked eastward to a broad sandy beach cut by two tidal rivers that drained the marsh. Waves gently roiled the sand and retreated, leaving a line of debris at high tide mark. The sweep of the waves tumbling in over the white stretch of sand carried a particular rhythm. Juanillo moved to its beat. His mother plodded beside him scanning the high-water mark.

From this awesome sea they soon saw they would gain little. To reap its bounty they would need a real boat. Most of the creatures cast up by the tide looked inedible. His mother grunted as she picked up a hard, pink mass. It could have been plant or animal, so strange was it to the Indians. She tossed it aside. Large, hard-shelled crabs shaped like horseshoes, bleached and empty shells, and sea cucumbers lay caught up in bundles of lacy, golden brown seaweed covered with small, amber, grapelike floats. None of the clawed crawlers and convoluted masses of jelly they stumbled across were recognizable to Juanillo or his mother.

Birds with large underhanging bills flapped in lines just above the water, riding up and down with each wave. Large and small birds plundered the waves, folding their wings to dive below the surface. They often missed but some broke the surface with small fish in their bills. A flock of tiny, yellow-legged birds scurried just ahead of the waves picking up small, hopping flealike creatures.

"Tomorrow we will go to the north and see if we really do have the island to ourselves. Look sharp for anything we can eat. The rice will not last long."

They started up the beach, walking, as the birds did, just ahead of the waves. Juanillo moved steadily along, only halfheartedly searching the bundles of seaweed cast up by the tide. They were passed by the great blue heron flying into the island's interior.

9

◇◇◇◇◇

The sun had almost completed its ride across the sky when mother and son again reached their campsite. The camp was nothing more than a bed of hastily gathered moss and the store of rice buried in a hole lined with leaves and covered with shells scavenged from the riverside.

They ate rice and pecans then settled down on the moss as the sun dipped below the horizon.

Juanillo awoke before his mother and crept silently from his pallet. Silently he stood under the largest oak tree near the river. His eyes scanned the sky for the great blue heron. Would the bird come again to feed at this spot? Did he follow the same pattern every day? Had the bird only just come to the island, too? Had they been fellow voyagers?

Just as dawn broke over the low trees on the hummocky

island the bird came across the river. He flew lazily and settled into the water, braking with his wings and dragging his feet. Then he folded his wings over his back and immediately thrust his bill into the water. When he withdrew it, a fish struggled crosswise in his bill. With a flip of his head the bird swallowed the fish head first and stood silently waiting for the next. Juanillo felt hungry and envious in his hunger. "Why isn't it easy for us too? Why do we always have to be hungry?" he mumbled.

His mother woke as he rattled the pecans in his quiver. He cracked several with the butt of his knife and handed them to her. Then he broke others for himself. The taste of the sweetmeats filled his mouth but made him thirsty. Still chewing he walked to the river and knelt to dip up water in his cupped hands. The river looked muddy. Juanillo hesitated for a moment, then tasted the water and spat it out. Salt! He had expected the river to be fresh and clear like the Ocmulgee that flowed by his farm.

"We will find fresh water," his mother said. "All this comes from the sea."

They started out to explore the north end of the island. As they left the clear park under the oak forest where they camped, the night feeders settled down to rest in hollow trees and burrows and the day feeders began moving about. The forest echoed with bird calls.

At a spot on the river bank some six feet above the water they came across a high mound that enclosed a large cleared area. Not far beyond lay another great mound, so overgrown and of such age that trees, each thicker than a man, grew atop it.

"I've heard of this place!" Juanillo's mother said. "It was the clearing where your forefathers the Guale camped. Here they held the ceremony of the 'black drink.' I tell you

[35]

this because it is your heritage. Always before battle the men cleansed their bodies with the black drink. The women prepared the drink out of certain shrubs and roots, which I have forgotten, and brought it to the men. The men drank, one after the other, and soon vomited. Some swooned. The drink purged them and made them brave, and in truth it seemed to have made them murderous, for they were always at war with someone — neighbors, Spanish, missionaries, English. Your forefathers didn't like the ways of the white man. They would not join his church. They would not take only one wife. They were a powerful nation, the Guale. But the nation fell and what few Guale survived joined with the Creeks many generations ago."

Juanillo listened to the singsong words spoken by his mother, but at the same time he heard oak leaves falling from the trees and the drumming of woodpeckers in the forest.

"It was white man that killed the Guale. Some by gun, but not all," his mother continued. "When they came here the white man brought diseases. Your forefathers died like flies from terrible sicknesses. So many were sick and dying, there was no one left to bury the dead. The Guale are all gone now, but we can bring a little life back to this deserted island.

"We should set our camp here. Perhaps the ghosts of our forefathers will protect us. There must be fresh water nearby," she added shrewdly. "This place is high. We can see across the channel if anyone approaches. And we can hide a fire in the depression. We cannot do better."

They walked on looking for the water they knew must be nearby. Soon they found a damp hollow near a pond. When Juanillo pressed the earth water seeped into the hollow.

His mother broke fronds from a palmetto, and with them she cleaned away the damp twigs and leaves. The water rose, sweet and clear — a spring.

"Now mark a tree!" his mother said. "So we can find it easily."

After the water had settled they drank their fill and started north again. They came to larger ponds and impenetrable growths of sharp-leaved palmetto with knotted, exposed roots. They could make little headway through the wild, tough plant, so they turned back toward camp. The north end of the island offered small help to them. They would have to gather their food from the woods and marshes of the south end and carry it to the mound. The animals would not have to share the wild part with them. The ibis and egret would roost undisturbed and the great blue heron would pass his quiet hours in solitude and mystery.

Juanillo and his mother would have little rest this day if they were to move camp. They walked back to the mound.

The woman gathered rafts of moss for their beds and cut palmetto fronds for shelter while Juanillo explored along the crest of the mound. He looked underfoot in a spot where an animal had been digging and saw something white. Curious, he dug with a stick and came across shells, hundreds of them. Quickly he ran to another spot and dug. More shells! And then to another spot.

"This whole mound is made of shells!" he shouted. "Is it possible? There must be more shells here than the sands of the beach!"

His mother came over to look. "I don't remember hearing about this in the old stories. Perhaps it was forgotten."

"But look! Now we will know what to eat for we will see what our forefathers ate."

[37]

"I named you well. Juanillo must be looking out for us," his mother said with a smile.

Juanillo dug quickly in the mound. Each time he came upon a new shell, he laid it carefully to one side. He found long, thin, knifelike shells and thicker heavy shells in the shape of a heart. He found spiraled shells as large as his two hands and shells no bigger than a fingernail. He dug further. Broken clay pots with black designs and large pierced shell disks turned up in the rubble. They must have been worn, Juanillo decided, for they looked like ornaments.

Long bones and skulls of deer lay in the mound. Bird bones, probably from ducks, so decomposed and powdery that they were almost unrecognizable, moldered with the shells. The mound was a gigantic kitchen dump. In awe and perplexity Juanillo tried to visualize all that was buried in this vast mound. His people must have come here for thousands and thousands of years, he thought to himself as he exposed layer after layer of shells and earth. These creatures would be their fare. The forefathers had shown them what to eat. Now they must show him where the animals lived.

Juanillo stood some time puzzling over the shells.

"We must go soon and get the canoe and bring it up river."

The boy was stunned. The canoe! He had forgotten their one link with civilization. His mind worked strangely on this island. He seemed able to keep only one thought at a time.

"I will get it," he said as he set off for the old campsite.

"No! Where one goes, the other goes, for we still don't know this place."

Juanillo waited for her to catch up though he felt he could have gotten the canoe alone. Within half an hour they reached the massive oak that had first sheltered them and to which they had tied the dugout. It was gone! The rope was old and had frayed a bit each time the waves rose and fell. Finally, it had broken and the canoe had floated away with the tide. Juanillo had not noticed it that morning as he stood searching the dawn for the great blue heron. Was the canoe there then or had it already floated away?

Despair showed in the woman's face. Her shoulders sagged.

"I'll make another canoe," Juanillo said quickly.

"It will take a long time." She frowned but seemed heartened by the idea. "How do we fell a tree suitable and how long will it take to burn and scrape? We will walk along the river. Perhaps we'll see the canoe and maybe some of the shells you found. We must eat."

Shells covered the river bank in such numbers that they grew atop one another, especially those white shells with sharp fluted edges that Juanillo found in abundance in the shell mound.

"These must be good to eat," Juanillo said as he tried to break a clump apart. The shells seemed melded into a solid heavy mass but some lumps contained only a few animals and came freely out of the mud. Juanillo washed them off in the river and studied how to break the shells apart. The animals inside had pulled the shells together tightly with a little hiss of expelled air. Juanillo tried to put the point of his knife in the shell, but this too was impossible. He threw a lump of shells against a tree. It fell unbroken to the ground. Was there no way to break the animal's hold? He tried chipping one shell against another. This worked. Soon he had chipped a hole large enough to insert his knife. By chance in his probing the knife blade severed the muscle that bound the shells together and Juanillo felt the animal relax. He tore one half of the shell off and curiously looked

[39]

inside. This was edible, this strange, gray, watery mass with a ruffled edge? How was it possible that such a slimy mass had defied his strength? He showed it to his mother.

"You have made no mistake? This is the same shell you found in the mound?"

"There can be no mistake. Most of the shells in the pile are like these."

They looked at the animal perplexed for a time, then Juanillo picked it up on the point of his knife and quickly put it into his mouth. In surprise he found that it had very little taste. A pleasant saltiness filled his mouth. He chewed a few times and swallowed the slippery mass.

He opened another shell and gave it to his mother. "We might even like these after a while," he said. His mother grimaced but she ate the offered oyster. Juanillo opened several more until they had eaten their fill. There was no sign of the canoe. They returned to camp.

The boy and his mother spent the rest of the day making a shelter of saplings tied together with thin, tough vines. The roof they thatched by overlaying the stiff palmetto leaves. In the middle of the roof they left a smoke hole so they could have a small fire to warm their sleep when nights became colder.

"This has been a good day's work," said his mother. "I am tired. The sun is almost down." She went inside the shelter to her thick nest of moss.

10

Instead of following his mother Juanillo walked to the riverside. He might see the heron on its flight homeward to the pond heronry. Juanillo scanned the sky flamed by the setting sun but it was empty of life. He then turned his attention to the river.

Rising water flowed upstream, lapping gently at the bank. Juanillo sat on a small rise and watched. At first he saw nothing in the motion except that water flowed from down near the sound at the south end of the island. Then he saw that the speed of the flow decreased as the mass of water moved upstream. Suddenly he realized that the river was a living thing, its body divided into different parts. Water moved fastest in the middle but dragged at the shoreline. He walked upstream for a bit until he came to a bend in the river. Here the fast-flowing, midstream water cut toward the outer bank where it slowed as it ate at the muddy bank of the opposite shore. Plumes of suspended mud fanned upstream on the current. Where the water cut back in a reverse curve, some of the mud settled against the opposite bank. He saw that in time the water would devour more and more of the bank, making an ever sharper bend which would finally become a circle. What would happen then he didn't know, for he could not see so far.

Juanillo knew he should return to camp but hunger gnawed at his stomach. The shellfish they had eaten seemed to have very little substance. He turned back downstream toward the shell bed near camp. It was now covered by the rising tide. He started to wade out into the river a short distance, carefully placing his feet so that he wouldn't step on the sharp shells. Quickly he sank in liquid mud which sucked and pulled at his legs. Within three steps he was hip deep. Desperately he tried to turn back and pull himself out of the ooze but each motion pulled him deeper and deeper in the dangerous mud. He knew he must stop struggling and thought to call his mother but was ashamed. He was caught like a small pebble in the river's power.

He stopped struggling and sank no deeper. A fear greater than that he felt when he had killed the trapper seized him. In desperation he gave the call of the screech owl he and his father had used when they had hunted together. Juanillo hoped the sound would carry to his mother and not be stilled by the breeze that blew off the river.

Whether his mother heard or not, Juanillo was conscious of her behind him. He heard the intake of her breath as she saw him waist deep in mud.

"I'll cut a vine and throw it to you. You must tie it around your chest. Then I'll pull." She was gone for a time, then came back as the last glow of twilight faded. Juanillo heard the hiss of the vine as it flew past his head. He missed it the first time. Lunging for it carried him deeper in the mud. On the second throw he caught the vine and tied it over one shoulder and around his chest.

His mother pulled. He churned his arms, washing mud into the stream. Each pull bore him up a little. Mother and son grunted and strained until their arms ached, but finally Juanillo lay on the solid ground of the bluff. He

[42]

gasped for breath. But when he had his fill of air he could say nothing. Shame stilled his tongue. Finally he got up and moved to the shelter. His mother followed.

. . . Next time I won't trust the river . . . Juanillo thought to himself. He lay on his pallet that night muddy and hungry.

The moon rose. Juanillo pulled aside the skin from across the door frame and looked out into the night. Here and there stars shown through openings in the mosaic of leaves overhead. He thought over the day's happenings and experienced once again the feeling of suffocating fear he felt as he sank in the mud. He slept hard on the heels of his thinking.

A curious dream came to him. In it he flew high in the sky alongside the great blue heron. On and on they flapped with powerful wings. Juanillo could see marsh grasses bending below them from the wind of their wing beats. But the grasses were withered and dried, not like the tall green leaves he knew. Then he awoke to the smell of smoke. His mother warmed her hands over a small twig fire. The night had passed.

"Today we will see what we can find in the white man's house." The security of their camp in the mound had erased some of her fear. "We will take our knives. And we should get as many pecans as we can carry."

They started on the same route that they had taken before. As they left camp, Juanillo saw the great blue heron flying in to land on the bank of the river. For a moment he remembered his curious dream but he couldn't fathom any more of its meaning in the daylight than he could the night before.

Still cautious, but bolder now, they walked the old wagon trail. Finally they entered the compound of the abandoned plantation. First they searched the slave quarters away from the main house and found little. A few shreds of cloth lay in dust-filled corners. These they carefully draped over their belts. An empty green glass bottle rested under leaves which had blown in through an open doorway. His mother put the bottle in her bag.

Together they went into the big house. Juanillo was so hungry he could taste the rich pecans which he knew were lying under the trees, but he put aside his hunger as his mother did.

The sun filtered through cracks in the wall and streamed through two broken windows. Alert to the dangers that might hover in the shadows, Juanillo overlooked the danger that lay almost underfoot. Suddenly he heard an ominous rattling. A huge rattlesnake undulated slowly as it coiled and uncoiled its wide body. Its flat diamond-shaped head spread larger than Juanillo's opened hand. The snake's forked tongue sensed the air with darting motions.

Juanillo stood completely still. He breathed slowly as the snake weaved his head from side to side. Then with sinuous movements the great serpent coiled. Juanillo felt no fear — only watchfulness. The snake had eaten, he could see, for its middle was much thicker than the rest of its body.

"Leave me in peace," the snake seemed to say. "I want to sun on these warmed boards. This is my territory! Beware!"

Juanillo relaxed along with the snake. He seemed to feel the length of its body as it slowly wound itself into a comfortable position. Then Juanillo felt himself inside the snake's skin, his ribs contacting the floor. He could feel a large rabbit inside him as coil piled on coil. Snakelike, Juanillo slipped through the door, hardly stirring the dust on the floor. Once outside the room, the snake feeling left him and once again he was a boy looking down at a power-ful, dangerous enemy, but the strange sensations had been slow to leave.

He did not tell his mother but cautioned her to watch for snakes. The last of the sensations slipped away as he again began the search for usable objects.

They found little in the main house. Had it been cleaned out by marauders or had the inhabitants left carrying all portable goods with them? Juanillo did find an iron pot which his mother seized. It was cracked and the handle broken out. Still it was a prize. A wooden bucket lay to one side of the kitchen hearth. A dark closet under the kitchen stairs yielded two flat bowls. The mother and son carried their prizes outside and filled them with pecans. They had to look longer, for the nuts were fast disappear-ing. Birds and squirrels scolded angrily as the Indians loaded the iron pot.

Burdened though they were, Juanillo and his mother stopped in the abandoned garden lying between the house and river. From the state of the trees and ground they could see that the garden hadn't been worked for several years. Already the forest marched to reclaim the portion that had been wrenched from it.

Juanillo's mother did collect the shiny, dark green leaves of a small holly tree, crushed a few in her hands, and smelled them. She collected more and put them atop the nuts. "These make good tea," she said. "Blackberry leaves too, if we find some."

The trip back to the shelter in the shell mound took three hours, for they had to stop and rest. They sat down and ate as many of the pecans as they wished. This was the last time they would do so for they would now ration a portion for each day.

11

◇◇◇◇◇

The days settled into a routine. Juanillo snared rabbits and shot the slow-witted opossums. The iron pot bubbled with meat stews. In the mornings Juanillo's mother heated up the remains of the stew from the night before. She always carefully covered the pot and set it in the crook of a live oak tree out of reach of at least a few of the night stalkers.

After they had eaten, she would busy herself picking up acorns which she broke open and let soak in baskets she had woven from palmetto. After repeated soakings she ground the acorns into flour. Some mornings Juanillo helped with the camp chores but some mornings he only watched from his pallet of moss. The two talked together less and less but the woman talked to herself more. Juanillo could see her lips move silently. Sometimes she remained in one spot for a long time whispering.

Some nights his mother talked aloud. She chanted the history of the Creeks and even before, the Guales. She remembered her girlhood and marriage, then recited the lineage of all the people she had known. Her singsong speech lulled him to sleep and she seemed not conscious of him.

Juanillo did not understand why she talked this way but he thought it strange.

After he had watched his mother in the mornings or

[46]

helped her, he would go off on his own to find food. Many hours he idled away tracking animals that he did not kill. He slipped over the ground on silent feet watching the animals go about their own business of seeking food. He shuffled about with them. He dug in the soft turf. He watched them settle in nests. He was like a ferret nosing out their secrets. More and more frequently he ended his day on the broad marsh.

Such days always seemed to begin with Juanillo's awareness of the herons growing restless on their night roosts. As dawn appeared in a faint line on the horizon, the birds would shift position on the tree branches, extend their necks from between hunched wings and begin their muted morning calls. A few would stretch their wings and fan them, warming up for the morning flight before settling back for a quick nap in advance of quitting the tree.

Egrets roosted with the herons. These white birds, like ghostly candle flames in the distance, sat through the night. Louisiana herons sat in company with the sleek black anhingas. Juanillo often saw them in faraway trees during the day, wings outstretched to dry for hours in the pale winter sun.

Like a monarch over all the others in the night roost, the great blue heron sat in the very top of a tree. All the birds would leave the roost and disappear to different parts of the island to feed. When the great blue heron winged over the camp, Juanillo was always ready. Together, but apart, they moved southward. Juanillo followed the large bird farther and farther over the marsh. These days the boy was gone from sunup to sundown.

On one such trip he found the canoe. It had washed down river and beached near high marsh. It was half sunk deep in mud. Juanillo tugged and pulled but couldn't get the bulky dugout to a stream big enough to float it. Then he began an anxious vigil to see that it did not wash away. When the tide ran full he struggled the canoe into the water and felt it float free. Two months in the mud seemed not to have damaged it although borers had gotten through its skin. The paddles were gone.

With his knife, Juanillo fashioned a paddle from an oak limb. The work took him two days. Then two more days were spent making another paddle. Another day was consumed in selecting a strong, light pole, which he used to push the canoe along near the banks of the shallow drainage creeks cutting the surface of the marsh.

For seven days he did nothing but paddle or pole through the creeks. He saw snails crawling up the grass stems to escape the rising water of high tide. They clung to the thin grass leaves which bent under the weight of the shelled animals. The snails looked like white blossoms in a field of swaying grass.

Juanillo came to know even the smallest and wariest marsh creatures, those that washed in and out with the tides and those that came from the uplands to feed on the marsh's surface. He watched a mother raccoon lead four young to a streamside. She prowled the muddy bank for a time. Then with a fast scoop she reached in the water and threw a fish onto the bank. It flopped around for a short moment before one of the young raccoons was upon it.

The mother raccoon ran quickly on small, black-tipped feet. With a peculiar chattering noise she warned the young away from the fish. She then broke its back while the young circled anxiously. She ate the fish and set off again. Soon she scooped another fish from the water and repeated the lesson.

One by one the young raccoons tried fishing. Two were skillful, the other two were much slower and learned only after trying to steal the others' fish. They were driven off with bared teeth and had to learn for themselves.

Suddenly the mother raccoon saw Juanillo. Alert, she stood in a defensive position. She drew her lips back over her teeth and growled. The peculiar feeling of being inside the animal came over Juanillo. He felt fear behind his alertness. His eyes remained steadily on the human who was Juanillo. His pulse quickened. The hairs on his body raised with a prickling sensation. He put the young raccoons behind him and prepared to defend them. Carefully he moved so that he was between them and the water. If he must he would swim and fight for he knew he had great strength in the water.

The mother raccoon turned suddenly and loped off, followed quickly by the four young. Juanillo shook himself and cursed. He saw dinner for the evening running through the tall streamside marsh grass. Still he could not bring himself to chase them down even though young raccoon would taste savory to his tongue. Shellfish would have to fill the pot again this night.

Darkness was gathering as Juanillo returned to camp. His mother was gone. Never before had she been out of sight of the clearing when he returned. Juanillo started to call her, then checked himself when he saw her still figure on the small bluff overlooking the river. He moved closer. Whether she heard or not she gave no indication but stood mumbling to herself. Juanillo could only catch a few words. They were of the farm, the killings, and her dead husband. She rambled out of her head.

Stricken with remorse, Juanillo took her by the hand and led her to the shelter. She seemed feverish, as she had after the birth of the dead child. He built a small fire and brewed tea of dried holly leaves. Quickly he gathered the familiar oysters and cooked a stew for the evening meal, thickening it with acorn flour. Then he carried it to her so she could eat inside the shelter. Soon after she fell asleep. For three days she lay in her bed of moss.

Juanillo stayed in camp watching over her as she lay mumbling. Gone was all thought of the great blue heron and the marsh. He did not search the skies for the familiar flapping figure. Instead he wove a net from thin vines.

For some time he had had an idea for a fish trap but he had whiled away the days. Juanillo reasoned that if he could weave a net long enough he could block one of the small marsh creeks. As the tide came in, fish and crabs entering on the tide could swim over the net. Then when the water receded and the animals tried to swim downstream, they could be caught. Fish enough for several days would end up on the spit over the fire or dried over tree limbs.

He did slip away long enough to try the net. It worked. His mother got up and set about smoking and drying mullet and menhaden for their store of food. She had awakened as if nothing had happened. To see her up made Juanillo's heart soar. His resolve to stay with her melted. He knew loneliness ate at her like a disease but the pull of the marsh proved stronger than his duty to stay with her.

12

Midwinter passed. Juanillo's breath hung frosty on the still, morning air. He shivered as he slipped into his buckskins. Then taking a dried fish and his bow and arrows he set out for the marsh. Before the pale morning sun rose he was in the canoe pushing off from the muddy creek bank.

It was near the mouth of the largest marsh drainage creek that he saw the biggest fish of his life. It lay in the water, the length of the dugout. The dolphin's dark upper body carried a fin about halfway to its tail. Its underbelly and lower jaw showed white against the muddy creek bottom. A peculiar humped head with a laughing mouth rose above the water. The fish wallowed and blew, making whistling, chattering noises. Suddenly a hole opened on the top of its head and Juanillo heard the intake of air. Then the great fish expelled a fine spray of moisture with the air.

Boy looked at beast and beast looked up at boy through shrewd eyes. In his mind Juanillo slipped into the fish's long body. He thrashed and pushed himself through the soft mud of the bottom of the creek.

As Juanillo crouched motionless a baby slipped out of the great fish. For a while it lay quietly beside its mother, then feebly began nursing at the breast by the tail. Juanillo rested as the beast rested. The baby gained strength during the day, nursing every fifteen minutes. Then as the tide turned and new water seeped into the creek, the mother and baby swam against the flow of water into the deep channel of the sound.

Juanillo turned back to reality. He beached his canoe as high on the creek bank as he could, carefully tying it to a log he had driven into the soft mud surface. He walked across the marsh, hurrying now to escape high tide. He stumbled on a terrapin moving along sluggishly, too cold to put forth even his usual slow speed.

Quickly Juanillo picked up the turtle to carry it back to

[51]

his mother. It would take the place of the raccoons he had let slip away. Turtle soup would fill their pot for two days. Why the terrapin moved on the marsh surface was a mystery, for it should have been sleeping, safely shrouded in mud. Perhaps it lived like the river turtles and some warmth had roused the sleeping animal from its nest.

As Juanillo moved over the sandy high marsh, swarms of tiny fiddler crabs scurried before his feet. He stopped to watch as the creatures cleaned the sandy surface with busy claws. The biggest ones had an enlarged claw that usually rested quietly on the sand. Occasionally one would raise a large claw in a threatening gesture, and another would move quickly out of the way.

Everywhere the crabs fed they left minute marks in the marsh surface where they had picked up mud and debris and put it in their mouths. Juanillo saw them sort through the mud diligently with fast movements of their mouth parts, then spit a ball of inedible stuff into their claw and put it back on the marsh surface.

The boy watched the crabs feed until high tide covered the holes they had dug in the sandy surface. The small crustaceans fed closer and closer to their burrows as the water rose. Just as water spilled over the lip of the holes the crabs dashed for home. Some stoppered the burrow with a plug of sand. Others used their heads as a stopper, breathing in an air bubble captured in the process.

Juanillo found a new shellfish in the marsh, one he had not seen on the river bank or beach. It bore a ridged, greenish shell and grew in large clumps directly in the mud. Around each clump the earth seemed higher. The lowest living animals were sunk in the mud. Many were dead. The newest, freshest animals grew near the top, ever pulling themselves upward by threads that came from between their shells.

All this information Juanillo stored in his mind. The whole structure of the marsh and the animals in it assumed their place in the pattern of nature. Juanillo saw that nature was a cycle. The grass grew. Animals ate the grass. Other animals ate the grass eaters. Some died on the marsh. Others were carried by tides out into the sound, where they were eaten. The food they had previously eaten and built into their bodies was carried out with them. The grass died and rotted on the muddy surface. Some bits of decayed vegetation floated out with the tides, some became embedded in the muddy surface. The grass died back during the winter. It would grow again the following spring from underground roots.

Juanillo returned to camp in a strange mood. It was as if he had solved a riddle.

Again Juanillo's mother did not stand by a welcoming campfire. The ashes of last night's fire lay white and cold. She was not standing under the big oak as Juanillo had found her when she became strange. Now she lay dreaming inside their makeshift shelter, her unseeing eyes wide open.

Juanillo kindled a fire and made a broth of the terrapin and some shellfish. When it was ready he took it to her and awakened her. She smiled and thanked him as she would have in the old times, but very soon she began talking in her singsong way. Juanillo couldn't tell if she chanted to herself or to him. The familiar wail of the past days filled the camp. She hardly noticed when he spoke. Juanillo knew he must now take care of her. He had become the stronger of the two. Her body and mind had watched over him all his years. Now it was his turn to care for her. Truly he had lost his baby name and had become a grown man.

"Tomorrow, and the day after, we will go together to the house. Maybe we'll find something we missed before,"

Juanillo said. His mother stopped chanting and struggled to pay attention to him.

"Yes. We will go to the house. The garden might still give us something although it is overgrown. I am truly getting tired of these shellfish."

Juanillo watched over her, talked to her, and lay awake long after she had sunk into sleep.

13
◇◇◇◇◇

The days grew longer. The sun arched higher above the horizon in its passage across the sky. Birds became restless. They flitted from branch to branch, singing loudly. Species Juanillo had never seen before appeared on the island as if from nowhere and distributed the breeding territories among themselves. The great blue heron did not fish every day. He seemed fat and uninterested. Some days he stood on the river bank with his head pulled between his wings. Other days he didn't appear. Juanillo himself felt restless.

One morning the wind carried an especially balmy hint of spring. Juanillo and his mother set off for the abandoned plantation. She carried a bag she had woven of palmetto leaves, always on the alert to gather food for their hoard.

The first find of food grew from the limb of an old oak. A large clump of a fluted, yellow mushroom lay like a jewel against the brown background. Juanillo easily climbed the tree, wrapped his legs around a large branch, and shinnied out to the mushroom. With his knife he cut half the mushroom off and left half. He let the cut half fall to his mother. She stowed it in her bag and smiled with satisfaction as Juanillo dropped to the ground.

Two deer bounded noisily away, startled by Juanillo and his mother. An opossum waddled slowly along on its way home after night feeding. Night herons flew ghostly in silence to their roosts.

Juanillo and his mother were approaching the avenue of trees leading to the abandoned plantation when Juanillo became uneasy, as if a shadow had passed overhead. Something about the place was different, something unidentifiable. Then it hit him. The plantation looked tidied. Branches that had fallen from the pecan trees and rotted where they lay were cleared away and piled behind the big house.

Juanillo grabbed his mother by the arm. She immediately read the danger signals. They moved slowly behind a tree and waited as they had the first day they visited the house. Nothing stirred. Juanillo signaled his mother to stay behind while he moved from cover to cover until he neared the house. Still no movement or sound came from within. He cautiously peeked through the rear door leading to the garden. Bundles and boxes were piled inside the house.

Fear struck Juanillo but it was a wary fear and not the panic of childhood. As quickly and quietly as he could he returned to his mother. Together they faded into the forest wall.

"People have come and left things. This means they will be back."

His mother had gained strength since Juanillo had been taking care of her, but her mind and resolve were still weak. She trembled as she blindly turned up island toward their camp.

"No! We will go this way!" Juanillo said as he pointed southward toward the marsh where he had spent many days learning the ways of the creatures. "If anyone comes today they will come to the landing here. We will be safe if we stay in the forest."

They walked quickly but silently until they reached the marsh border. There they waited under the oak trees hung with moss until afternoon faded into evening. Then Juanillo led his mother to the concealed canoe. She looked silently at him for a moment but did not reproach him.

Juanillo helped his mother into the dugout. Each took a paddle and pushed off in the waning daylight. An increasing moon lit their way past the plantation and on to the camp.

14

Juanillo dozed but little. Apprehension filled his mind and he dreamed. Again he and the great blue heron flew above the earth. Together they winged their way along the river. Then the heron drew ahead with powerful wing beats while Juanillo fell behind, his wings weakened. Then he realized they weren't wings at all but arms. He felt himself falling and woke up. The night was warm and moist. The din of spring peepers filled his ears. Yet he trembled as he had during the coldest night of winter.

He got up in the predawn darkness and stood like a statue under the protective oak on the bank near the canoe. They must leave with the dawn and be out in the sound before full light. Juanillo waited, as he had so many times during the winter, for the great blue heron. His coming would be an omen for good, but the boy waited in vain.

Fingers of dawn reached over the horizon. Still the bird did not come. His mother stirred, got up, and came toward Juanillo. "Is it time?" she asked. Juanillo looked at the tide running downstream and nodded. They would have to leave.

Both got into the dugout and settled themselves for the long paddle ahead. With burning eyes and an ache in his throat Juanillo dipped his paddle in the water.

As they pushed the canoe downstream Juanillo looked from side to side, seeing where he had adventured and learned the ways of the island. Silently he thanked the trees for providing shelter and food. He thanked the marshes for sustaining them through the winter. He cast his eyes back for a final search of the sky for his bird.

It came flapping lazily behind them as the dugout reached the mouth of the river. For a short time they paralleled each other, then as Juanillo and his mother pointed the canoe toward the sound, the great blue heron turned northward to follow the wide, strong river. For as long as he could see the bird Juanillo's mind soared along in flight. Finally the great blue heron disappeared against the rising morning sun.

On the horizon Juanillo saw a boat so distant it looked like a toy. Juanillo knew from its length that it was a large dugout canoe. It was coming from the mainland.

[57]

A man stood in the bow. On each side of the canoe the boy counted six oars dipping and flashing in the new sun. The canoe towed a flat barge on which machinery was lashed. With strong, regular strokes the large dugout moved toward the island.

Juanillo and his mother bent hard over their paddles and disappeared in one of the trough of waterways leading from the sound, their course set southward where they would join the Seminoles, their family kin, in the broad Florida Everglades.

Part Two

15

◇◇◇◇◇

The great blue heron flew northward. Unlike the steady flight south, the northern journey was broken. He settled into marshes and creeks along the flight path for days at a time, following the advance of spring as it slowly moved up the coast.

Pamlico Sound reflected his still figure as he stood knee deep in water. Then taking flight, still northward, he stopped to fish the small rivers emptying into Delaware Bay.

The heron could have stayed all summer at any spot along the way but he was drawn ever northward to the Gloucester marsh from which he had flown months before.

From Delaware Bay he winged his way in two stages to the tip of Long Island. Here he stopped again, for he had advanced faster than the spring season. The fishing was good in the shallow waters of the creeks. He stayed until the daylight hours lengthened and the breezes, which ruffled his gray-blue feathers, grew warmer. Then once again he moved northward.

Familiar landscape passed beneath him. Powerful wing beats carried him onward, following the calendar of the sun that directed his life. Past Boston Harbor he flew. Spits of land and rocky shores fell away beneath him.

Small harbors opened up here and there. Ahead lay the knob of Cape Ann. He skirted Gloucester Harbor and then winged a little farther inland, where an occasional house lay tucked in a clearing in the woods. Here and there a cow grazed in upland pastures.

The great blue heron flew over a narrow, rutted dirt roadway down which a two-wheeled cart, drawn by an emaciated horse, wound its slow way. A tall, lean man with deep furrows down both cheeks held the reins in rough, thick hands. His wife sat beside him, the fringe of her black shawl jiggling each time the ancient horse took a step. In the back a young girl, dressed in a tight-fitting cap and long linsey-woolsey gown, lay on some loose hay. Boxes and chests hedged her in so that she hardly had room to move. Her head drooped and though she fought to keep her eyes open, sleep caught her. The illness she had suffered on the voyage had left her exhausted and weak. The captain, who had given her a potion from the ship's medicine chest, said she was lucky to be alive.

The man tugged at the reins and the nag stopped before a derelict house on a hillock overlooking a creek that wound its way through a broad salt marsh. A flock of herring gulls took noisily to the air, wheeling and flapping toward the ocean front.

Just as the heron touched down on the mud of the creek bank, the man lifted the young girl over the back of the two-wheeled cart and set her on wobbly legs. The woman climbed down from the seat in front.

The lanky man turned his attention toward the house, but the girl looked with awe and fear at the great bird. Then with stiff movements she moved after her father. A pallor lay on her pinched cheeks. She shivered even though the breeze that touched her face was warm. Her body was painfully thin due to the small rations meted out to her on the eight-week voyage and the fever that had burned for a week through her young body. Her blue eyes were dull and half covered by drooping lids. But even her fatigue and thinness could not mask the promise of beauty on her face.

Once more she turned back to look over her shoulder at the heron. She saw him settle and preen his feathers, then fold his wings over his back. She saw that he was beautiful, but the recognition did not remove the fear that lay behind her eyes. The bird had come upon her so fast as she lay in the cart that she had stopped breathing for a moment.

The girl had never been so close to a wild animal in her life. She knew only mangy curs that roamed town streets with their tails between their legs. She had seen cats and rats as big as young dogs scurrying through refuse-lined alleys. She had seen pigeons flap from building to building, but she had never seen any bird as large and majestic as the great blue heron.

It had been with haughty grandeur that the bird alighted. It was as if he had dropped down to establish his supremacy, to claim his territory, to warn her off the broad salt meadow. As the woman called the girl, the great bird took to the air and flapped off slowly.

"Emily! Don't wander away now."

Emily walked unsteadily to a big rock near the cart and sat down.

Her mother turned with sagging shoulders toward the man. She reached inside her pocket for a cloth and coughed into it. Her cheeks flamed.

"Elias Wentworth! Are you sure there's no mistake? This could not be our house. It just could not be! We must find our place and get Em to bed. And I could use a place to put my weary bones."

[63]

Elias pointed a work-splayed finger dumbly at a spot on the crude map he held. "This is it, right enough. There's no mistake. This is our house." Like his wife he stood with sagging shoulders.

With their hands held awkwardly at their sides, the two looked perplexed at the crude building, more shack than house. The sides were dressed here and there with shingles but as many areas remained uncovered as covered. Part of the roof was off and they could clearly see into the house through the hole where the door should have been.

"But what could have happened?" Mary Wentworth asked in a shocked voice. She pressed her eyes with her hand to shut out the dismal sight.

The deep lines from his nose to his mouth drew tight as Elias said, "We've been swindled, that's what! That scoundrel took our money and said he would put it into a good house for us. Instead he's given us a hovel not fit for pigs!"

He did not raise his voice but Emily and Mary caught the suppressed rage behind the quiet voice, rage against the nephew who had bilked them of the money it had taken the family years to accumulate, a farthing at a time. Pain and frustration had earned the farthings, and hope had saved them, hope for a new life in a new country.

Elias Wentworth's life had been ruled by hardship and pain and deprivation. Apprenticed at ten to a bootmaker, he had spent seven years in the cellar of the master's shop with only the light of a grilled window and a feeble candle to work by. When he was apprenticed his body was sturdy, for he had been raised on a farm owned by a lord. He had drunk milk, eaten eggs and vegetables, not always as much as he wanted, but enough to give his body strength.

The family of mother, father, five boys, and four girls lived in a thatched cottage with an attached stone barn. In the churchyard lay six other children, stillborn or dead of childhood diseases, their graves marked by small stones. If he had not been naturally strong Elias would have succumbed to rickets or some other disease of deprivation.

For seven years of servitude he received room, such as it was — a mat on the floor of the dark cellar — and board, such as it was — bread, rank beef or mutton once a week, pease porridge, tea, and a pint of ale on Sundays.

When his time was served he had a few cobbling tools from his master, skill in leather and fit, and the round shoulders he would carry through life.

Ten more years passed while he worked as journeyman cobbler for those who would have him, earning barely enough to feed himself. He did not stay long in a town for he was generally considered sullen. He wanted always to put his tools away and hit the highway for parts unknown. But always at the end of his dreams lay a farm. Finally, his private dream became an overwhelming desire.

Yet ten more years passed. He married. When he had courted Mary he had talked to her glowingly of his plan to move to America. Mary had brought little enough in the way of a dowry to the marriage but she had a clear head and frugal ways. She began putting aside the coppers and farthings that eventually paid their passage.

Mary lacked the natural hardiness of her husband. When she was brought to bed with Emily she nearly died, but she and the child survived. Emily, though small, cried lustily when she was born. No more children followed.

Mary looked older than her years, older than Elias. She covered decayed and missing teeth with her hand as she spoke. She coughed frequently from the consumption that ate at her lungs. She was frequently down with fevers but she had managed to work toward their dream of a farm.

When the box that held the family's treasure was nearly full, Elias took the step of writing to a nephew in Massachusetts to look for land for them.

The glowing descriptions that had been written to the family about the house being built on a nice piece of high ground leading down to a salt marsh were more fancy than fact, but at least the farm appeared to be fertile. Even now, with spring just beginning, the marsh bore the suggestion of fresh green around the bases of the grasses. The upland had been partially cleared and showed promise. The house, derelict though it was, rested between two tidal creeks.

On the broad marsh last year's growth of grass lay in matted patches. Alders and baybushes lined the borders between upland and marsh. Birds had long since picked the bayberries clean of last fall's crop, but soon blossoms would cover the grayed plants and, in late summer, the waxy, greenish berries would mature into white clusters.

Long-legged birds probed the mud of the tidal creeks. From across high dunes bordering the shore nearby came the plaintive call of gulls and terns as they wheeled about the sky. Quarrelsome herring gulls fished and reeled across the sky pursuing those with fish in their bills. The pursued birds wheeled away in desperate moves to keep their prize. The weakest opened their bills and the pursuers darted after the falling fish.

Emily drew back from the spectacle of nature before her and tried to block out the calamity that had befallen the family. As she looked from the house to the marsh she didn't know which frightened her most — the strange open space without cover or the creatures, especially the monarch bird who had seemed to fix a stern eye on her as he flew past. She had seen his long bill clearly. It was sharp enough to cleave her skull if he chose. The low marsh

[66]

looked as if it would swallow her, dared she put her feet on its sucking, shiny surface. Terrors of the unknown ate at her mind and she feared even the innocence of nature.

16
<><><><><>

When they first cast off from England, Emily's mind raced to their destination. Then time slowed her thoughts. Seconds and minutes and hours ticked slowly by in dismal procession. The deck of the ship was forbidden when the ship pitched and rolled, which was most of the time. Waves and spray often washed over the bow. The Wentworths were confined to a cabin the size of a closet. Lying seasick in their bunks, Mary and Emily squeezed into one, Elias bent almost double in the other, the family despaired of ever reaching their destination. They feared for their lives as the schooner groaned, reared, and plowed through the giant waves churned by late winter storms.

Emily regained her feet first. On a calmer day she had gone out on deck while Mary and Elias rested in the bunks. During her short turn of freedom Emily had poked about every corner of the deck, looking in awe at the block and tackle which groaned as great lines were pulled through them.

She had talked with a sailor who smiled at her with cracked and caked lips. His eyes had burned bright. Sweat-dampened hair had clung to his forehead. He told her of voyages to India, of strange marketplaces and foods and costumes.

Two weeks later Emily fell ill. Mary fought to nurse her, but the captain, fearing an outbreak of the disease among the passengers and crew, removed Emily to a small cabin where he and a dull cabin boy could attend her needs. Mary and Elias raged at the captain from outside the locked door, but they were not allowed inside. Emily passed one week in delirium and high fever and two more recovering. Only then was she allowed out of the cabin and into her parents' care. She sat on deck, swaddled in a coarse woolen blanket, and watched the waves break against the hull of the ship.

At last they approached Gloucester. Yellow-backed sand dunes marked the horizon. Two spits of land protected a natural, deep, rock-lined harbor where other ships lay at anchor. Ahead were the wharves, visible first as only a blur of masts sticking up from the packets, whalers, barks, and schooners that lined them.

As their ship furled her sails the seamen stood by with lines ready to throw around piles and pull the ship in to dock. Emily stood on the bow longing for the moment she would once again step on solid earth, no matter how foreign. Line zinged through the air and hit with a thud on the cob and ballast wharf.

Emily could hear the strike of hammer on iron from shore and the rumble of drays being loaded and driven off by thick-bodied men who cracked long whips over the backs of oxen. Smaller boats lay at anchor with nets strung from the masts. Bales covered with India jute cloth lined the dock. Piles of baleen and barrels of whale oil stood on the deck of a whaler nearby.

The arrival of the schooner created a commotion on the

dock. The owner had come to meet the ship and congratulate the captain on his safe arrival. Well he might, for his fortune lay in the holds of the ship: bales of silks and cottons from India and porcelain and stoneware made in the potteries of Staffordshire. The owner was to board the ship for the rest of the journey to Boston to deal directly with merchants who came to buy his cargo.

The docks were busy. Bricks were being unloaded and wide pine boards put in their place on other ships tied to the Gloucester wharf. Barrels of salted cod were being rolled onto ships. Haddock and flounders were being forked from fishing vessels into carts and trundled off to Gloucester center. The bustle enlivened Emily, but when she finally did step on the dock she nearly fell, feeling she must brace herself against the pitch of a dock that didn't move.

Elias rented a two-wheeled cart pulled by an ancient horse. Even though she felt dizzy, Emily managed to help load boxes and bags into the cart. She was only too happy when they at last finished and she settled gratefully on the hay in the back of the cart.

The shipowner paced the deck nervously, for he and the captain wanted to catch the tide and favorable wind out of the harbor. The family watched as their home — their prison for eight weeks — cast off.

Elias helped Mary onto the box seat in the front of the cart, climbed on himself, and took up the reins. So began the final stage of the journey toward their new home. On either side of the rutted Essex Road lay ponds, lakes, tideways, woods, and salt marshes. Houses dotted the landscape. For an hour they jounced slowly along. The day's excitement had kept Emily awake, but now she drowsed even though she jerked from side to side with the motion of the cart. Finally, after consulting his map, Elias turned off onto a cartway cut through the trees and the family stopped to confront their calamity.

"Yes, there's nothing for it but to go inside the house," Elias echoed Mary.

Emily cast an apprehensive look toward the marsh to see if the great bird had reappeared, but the broad salt meadow was empty. Emily followed her parents inside the house. A startled bird flew through the hole in the roof. A small animal scurried through a burrow under the foundation of granite blocks.

Tears welled in Mary's eyes as she looked around. Work to be done confronted the family on every turn. Fortunately a good fireplace had been built into one end of the main room. Two other small rooms led from the main room. These had no fireplaces, but they also had no doors. The full warmth of spring had not yet arrived, so the family would still have to lay fires to ward off the evening chill.

"Well, crying will have to come later!" Mary said briskly. "This house may not be what we expected, but at least it is shelter. Emily, you might find some branches for a fire. Your father and I will bring the boxes inside."

Emily picked up the small fallen twigs and branches that lay about the clearing around the house. This supply soon ran out. She looked toward the nearby woods where she was sure she would find kindling aplenty under the trees, but the long shadows inching toward the house from the woods frightened her. Fear of the unknown lurked in those long shadows. She turned toward the marsh. She remembered having seen wood caught in rafts of grass stalks along the creek bank. Anger at having to choose between two fears stopped her and brought tears to her eyes. Again she looked at the darkening forest and then walked

unsteadily down the small hill in front of the house toward the winding creek.

She hesitated on the brink of the marsh. Then she half stepped, half jumped from the swell of the upland down onto the mat of old marsh grass. Water seeped quickly around her boots to cover the toes, then the first button. Hurriedly she stepped forward. Here the water was not so deep, but she felt the mat of marsh grass stir beneath her.

Emily could hold back her tears no longer. She cried bitterly as she threw together a pile of boards and branches and grabbed them against her chest. She gave up trying to find a dry spot on the marsh surface. Her boots were soaked through. Her bonnet fell off the back of her head. Soil from the boards and branches worked its way into her linsey-woolsey dress.

Through tears she caught the second glimpse of the great blue heron who fished placidly behind a small knoll. The bird calmly looked over the marshscape, then turned his head toward her. Emily watched him warily. So strong was the feeling that the marsh belonged to the bird that inwardly she asked, "May I trespass?" The bird ruffled his feathers, threw his neck forward, and resumed fishing, leaving her question unanswered.

She stood watching the bird until the tears stopped coursing down her cheeks. A tremulous peace settled over her. From that moment the bird became her talisman, just as he had been Juanillo's. The two young people, who would forever remain unmindful of each other's existence, were linked by the solitary great blue heron, a bird of passage who touched both lives. To Juanillo he had been an omen, a brother. To Emily he was a challenge. No matter how hard the task, she determined to be as at home in the new, frightening surroundings as the bird was. No matter how odious the marsh now seemed, she told herself it would at last become hers. Emily's brave thoughts did not fully cast out the fear of the open marsh that, like a live thing, sucked and pulled at her feet with every step. She was happy to put it behind her as she lugged the wood back to the house. A shadow passed over her as the great bird once again took flight.

The rest of the day was spent sweeping out the house with a makeshift broom of tall, wiry grasses which Mary had collected from the dunes and tied together. Elias cleared the well behind the house and brought in a bucket of clear, sweet-tasting water. Gratitude overwhelmed Emily. Water had never tasted so good. She drank deeply from the dipper. As the clear liquid ran down her throat, it washed away the husky feeling that had lodged there since the family had first seen the house.

Emily was sent to the marsh once more to cut and bring as much of the fine salt hay as she could carry to stuff coverlets which her mother had hastily sewn together. These would have to do for mattresses. The sun was beginning its descent. Still reluctant, but less so this time, Emily started down the hillock.

For supper the Wentworths ate a porridge of cornmeal and molasses brought out from Gloucester with a three-legged iron pot to cook it in. The family lay down together in their clothes on the mattress before the fire and fell into the sleep that visits the exhausted.

The next day Elias drove the cart into town and brought back pine boards, nails, and small panes of glass, even though the price of the last was very dear. The boards took shape as doors and the glass was carefully fitted into window sashes with eight-over-eight panes.

With the amount of work to be done, day followed day

in rapid succession. Emily could see two other houses some distance up the river that snaked through the marsh. Each farm had its haystacks resting on stakes driven directly into the muddy surface. Occasionally she would see figures, small in the distance, and longed for them to wave to her. But they went about their business and she was forced to get on with hers.

17

In May the marsh grasses grew rapidly. The roots had been safe, protected under the muddy surface from ice packs which rode up and down on the tides, shearing off last year's stalks. Now new green shoots poked their way through the mat of dead grass. The marsh became a verdant meadow of salt hay. Along creek banks the taller thatch grass grew even more vigorously.

Elias gathered the thatch and spread it out on the upland to dry. Then he bundled it, cut the stalks off evenly, and laid the bundles in layers on the roof, covering the holes and shingles. He whistled a tune as he worked steadily. Emily paused in gathering firewood. She had never heard her father whistle before. When Elias had finished, the house resembled the thatch-roofed cottage of his boyhood. His heart eased as he looked at his handiwork.

"I do believe this is the same kind of grass we thatched

with back home, or nearly like," Elias said to Mary as they ate a crude meal of corn dodger, molasses, and tea. "Isn't that a wonder! Could it be we left one place to come to another just alike?"

"Maybe the difference ain't as great as it could be, but here we have our own place. Back home you could never be anything but servant to the bootmaker."

"I ain't complaining, you understand. Just remarking that things ain't so different. Makes it easier to work, knowing what you're dealing with."

"Well, bread's always the same and if I don't get a batch set we won't have any for the day."

Mary called Emily to help. As they poured sugared water in a bowl over the yeast Mary had carefully nurtured she said to Emily, "There's a wealth of food in that marsh. It only wants to be gathered. There's shellfish and birds. If you look sharp you can find eggs, too." Together they worked flour into the mixture. When it was still fluid but gummy they added salt and grease. After working in more flour until the dough was stiff and came away from the sides of the bowl, they covered it with a cloth and put the dough to rise in the sun.

"My mother used to get pickles made from samphire that grew in the marshes back home," Mary continued. "Maybe it grows here too. And there's marshmallow. For that you look for a big pink flower, as big as a saucer. Then you pull the roots and boil them. When the liquid gets thick, you put it in a bottle and cork it. It's good for coughs and other winter ailments. We made sweets from it too. I think I remember my mother putting honey with the mix and stirring and mixing until it got creamy. Now that's a real treat. Look for it!"

The prospect of going, once again, into the marsh, even for something that sounded as enticing as marshmallow, didn't appeal to Emily. Actual fear had lessened but she still mistrusted the open space.

Not many days later a great number of birds, especially black-bellied plovers, calico plovers, and longer-billed brown shorebirds, joined the great blue heron on the marsh. The birds flew in large flocks. The rustling noise of their flight and calling first reached Emily's ears as she drew water. She shaded her eyes with her hands and stopped to watch the birds settle on the surface, rise up and wheel and turn as new individuals joined them. Awe for the spectacle paralyzed her. Then she saw her father drop his work and run into the house.

Elias reappeared with his musket and powder horn and hurried down to the marsh. Black-bellied plovers flew off warily and took many of the calico-colored birds with them. But other calicos and the long-billed birds sat, unmindful of danger. Elias loaded the gun with shot and powder, put it to his shoulder, and fired into the mass of birds. They rose in the air with a rush of wings only to move a short distance and settle again. Elias reloaded and fired once more. Wings flashed in the sun.

Elias could not control himself in the face of such bounty and fired again and again, almost in a frenzy. All about the marsh lay fallen and dying birds. Then he felt ashamed of the carnage and guiltily picked up as many of the birds as he could carry and took them back to the house, where he and Mary dressed them. From the distance came the firing of other muskets. That night Emily ate so much of the unaccustomed meat that she felt ill.

Each day now Emily went to the marsh. With each rising and setting sun she felt more comfortable in the strange open salt meadow. Without realizing it she had broadened her range to the shore where waves washed over jumbled rocks. Lining the rocks were vast numbers of blue-shelled mussels, so plentiful that they grew atop one another. She took an apronful of the shellfish home to ask her mother if they were edible. Mary took the blue shells, put them in the pot in the fireplace with just a little water, covered the pot, and steamed them until they opened, revealing the orange-colored animal within. Emily discovered for herself that they were delicious.

One day while walking barefoot on the mud flat between ocean and marsh Emily stepped down with her heel on something hard lying under the mud surface. She saw two small holes side by side. With a small stick she dug down into the soft mud and soon unearthed a large, heavy shell as big as her two fists together. This she carried home too. Elias looked at it in surprise. He had never seen a shellfish so large, even on the fishmongers' carts in England. He forced the shell apart with his knife and sniffed. Cautiously he put his finger into the liquid inside the shell and tasted.

"My girl," he said. "This is a good day's work. You might look for more. It wants boiling but it's got a very good flavor." Emily went to the mud flat again and worked through it with her bare feet in search of more quahogs.

The family's menu was catch-as-catch-can, but it was nourishing and more plentiful than they had gotten at home. Enough of the upland had been cleared for Elias to turn up a bit of garden. After a trip into Gloucester to buy seeds he carefully counted his money. For a long time that night he sat staring into the fire. The family's small supply of cash was fast running out. The expense of rebuilding a house they thought already completed reduced their store of money drastically. The money for a cow and a few chickens had gone to the sawmill for boards and to the hardware for cut nails. They had to buy a few staples: salt, sugar, flour and coffee.

Then came the week the money completely ran out.

Mary's cheeks flamed as Elias told her that they didn't have a copper in the world. Instead of berating him, Mary turned her anger against the nephew who robbed them.

"Oh, don't I wish he were here right now! Maybe it's just as well he ain't. I don't think he would survive the drubbing I'd give him!" For the next few minutes, dust flew in clouds under her vigorous sweeping.

"We all have to find what food we can," Elias said. "I'll hunt for market. Maybe I can trap, too. We shouldn't starve here, but we'll really have to dig!"

Talk of the money running out frightened Emily. They had always been poor and watched pennies, but they had never been stone cold broke before. One more fear to add to her growing burden. She occasionally longed for the familiar streets of home where she knew every nook and cranny. She longed for her friends. Loneliness crowded in on her at times while she bent over her work. She cried privately. Occasionally she heard her mother do the same when she thought she was alone.

More and more often now Mary grew short of breath and had to sit down. Her cheeks glowed with an internal fire. Her eyes shone, or rather, glistened. More and more often, Mary coughed into a cloth she carried in her apron pocket. Emily thought her mother had never been prettier, not realizing that the healthy glow was a deception. But Emily did see that the cloth was often spotted with blood when Mary hastily put it back into her pocket.

Mary tried to keep the blood-flecked cloth hidden from Elias too. He in his turn pretended not to notice. But he looked at her frequently and then dropped his eyes. He read the signs of advanced consumption. They both knew there was nothing to do and in a silent pact held their tongues.

For relief from the tense house, Emily took more and

more to the marsh, leaving her mother resting or working slowly. Each time Emily went down the hill toward the creek she remembered her misgivings and shadowy fear. Once on the marsh surface her eyes sought its wonders. She marveled as new sprouts of salt hay worked their way upward. Almost daily she could see it grow. And with its growth new animals appeared.

Crickets chirruped and hopped about through the thick mat of last year's fallen grass. Spiders wove gossamer webs between stalks to catch newly hatched insects. Snails trailed over the marsh, leaving minute tracks on the surface. As the tides rose they climbed the grass stems and remained swaying on the slender leaves like white blossoms until the water receded. Always in the background was the presence of the great blue heron, not always visible, but stalking or standing silently by the hour as breezes blew the fringed feathers on the back of his head.

Killdeer moved into the marsh. Emily could see the two black breast bands clearly as the birds bobbed their heads with each step. When they took to the air, the rusty patch at the base of their tails gleamed in the sunlight. Meadow larks flocked onto the salt marsh to feed on the emerging insects.

Once when she was very quiet, Emily saw a bittern, its thin head thrust outward as it stalked the streamside. Its streaky brown body appeared now and again as it slipped between the tall thatch plants.

Early one morning before the sun rose above the fresh-smelling earth, Emily slipped out of the house to sit near the marsh. The world lay in silence. She sat quietly on a rock eager to catch the first rays of the sun.

From a distance the great blue heron came flapping his way toward her. The bird settled on an open area, a sort of

stage, high above the rest of the meadow, and pulled his
wing feathers through his long bill. Emily watched curiously. Then from a different direction came another heron
and then a third from still another direction. Within half
an hour eight birds had assembled on the marsh plot. They
began posturing and flexing their wings. Some rose in the
air and circled around one another. Then all rose and
flapped slowly up and down in a wide circle. Again they
landed on the marsh. Some of the birds walked around
with great dignity while others croaked to them in an invit-
ing manner. Emily knew that the stalkers were male and
the croakers female just as she knew her father was a
man and her mother a woman.

Emily watched as her heron stalked toward a female.
Before he reached her another male rushed with wings
outstretched and bill thrust forward, trying to drive him
away. Emily could feel a slight vibration on the rock as
bird thrust at bird, each parrying and counterthrusting like
swordsmen. Her heron's crooked bill seemed no detriment
for he knocked his rival to the ground. The fallen bird lost
interest in the female and limped away ruffling his feathers.

The sun rose higher. Pink dawn turned into lemon-
colored morning. Emily's heron and another left separately
but headed in the same direction. Soon, one by one the
other herons rose and flew away, passing on their mysteri-
ous way to places Emily had never been, to heronries
hidden from human eyes.

Emily heard her mother call from the house. Time to
begin another day. Still she sat musing on the rock. Her
fear of the marsh continued to slip away. She felt a kin-
ship with the open space now, a part of it. Her face was
brown in the sunlight. Her arms, pitifully thin when the
family arrived, were now strong. The illness that had

[79]

stamped her face so harshly was completely erased. It mattered less that she had yet to meet her first playmate. The birds became her companions. Her mind rambled over the countryside. She talked to rabbits that hid in the growing grass. She called to swallows darting over the marsh.

When large flocks of shorebirds settled nearby she sometimes clapped her hands just so she could watch them fly off and wheel about before settling back on the surface. Some birds appeared fearless. She could approach quite close before they flapped off or walked ahead of her.

Emily's day usually began by bringing in firewood while Mary exposed the embers from the fire of the night before. If it had died, she rekindled it with a flint stone and a bit of dried moss. While her mother laid the fire Emily drew a bucket of water for the breakfast of porridge and coffee. After breakfast came the drawing of more water for washing up.

The two then swept, dusted, and made the beds, which meant they picked up the mattresses. On fair days they draped the stuffed ticking coverlets outside over a fence. On wet days they stowed them in the corner. They then washed the bare plank floor. Where grease had splashed from the three-legged cooking pot they rubbed the wood with a soft pumice stone. It was after these chores that Emily went to the marsh to look for food to fill the midday pot. Each day she searched for the heron but he did not appear. His absence distressed her and she wondered where he had taken himself off to.

Emily learned to set snares for marsh rabbits. She knew where mice tunneled through the grass mat, where plant hoppers were most abundant, where fish came most often into the creek. She found crabs living in the rocky shore beyond the marsh entrance. These she lured with a fish head tied to a string. She threw the head into the water and waited until a crab swam over to the bait. When the crab caught hold Emily carefully pulled the fish head and crab to the bank, where she scooped them up in a pail. Six crabs made a good meal and twelve a feast. Emily got very good at cooking and picking the tasty crab meat from the body and legs.

One day, after the chores were finished, she lay on her stomach on her rock, warming like a lizard in the sun. As she looked into the water she saw a fish. It headed upstream to the great pond that terminated the end of the creek. She thought little about it, content to watch the fish as it worked its way along. But within a few minutes she saw three more, and then more than she could count. Her eyes opened wide. She climbed down from the rock and ran to the house.

"Mother, Mother! Come see! There is a great run of fish in the stream!"

Mary looked up from washing clothes in a wooden tub in the yard. Taking her hands from the water she wiped them on her apron. "What is it?"

"You have never seen so many fish. There must be hundreds. They just keep coming!" Mary ran to the streamside, breathless from the exertion. Together she and Emily watched the fish, one after another, slip upstream with the incoming tide.

"There, my girl, is our winter meat. These and the birds. Hurry, we must catch some."

Emily ran back to the house. Mary followed slowly, calling to Elias, "Do come help! The herring are running. Have we a barrel? Have we enough salt? We must put some down for the winter."

The family quickly gathered two buckets and a pot and

carried them to the streamside. They had only to dip into the water and scoop the fish out. When they had worn themselves out with scooping and throwing, they were drenched, but hundreds of fish lay flopping and dying on the marsh. All that afternoon Elias, Mary, and Emily sat beside the stream scaling and gutting the fish. Emily cut her fingers several times on the sharp spines along the fish's belly. She could hardly keep tears from her eyes as salt-water ran into the cuts. The two lung-shaped masses of pink eggs from the female fish went into a bucket to be fried for supper that night. By evening Emily had seen and held enough slippery fish to last her a lifetime.

The gutting and filleting attracted flocks of gulls who fought and chased each other for scraps, even though large piles of offal remained untouched.

That night Mary could not sleep. Her eyes glowed. Elias looked anxiously at her as she sat up, trying to catch her breath. She coughed violently into her cloth. While Emily slept, Mary hemorrhaged. The cloth was soon drenched. Elias fetched a basin, but before Mary lay back exhausted, the basin was half full of frothy blood.

18

Mary no longer rose with the sun. She lay abed ill. As day followed day, Emily was forced more and more inside herself. Her father turned all his attention to his wife. Emily didn't even have her talisman, the great blue heron, for company. His familiar shadow did not pass over the marsh.

The heron and his mate had taken up residence in the same nest, forty feet above ground, used by his old companion, the heron who had been shot. The heronry in the tall spruce trees became like a busy village as pairs of birds moved in to set up housekeeping. The great blue heron had to challenge another male for the nest, but the defense was halfhearted. Other unused nests lay close by.

The herons mated several times. The nest was lined with fresh, fine twigs and the female laid the first egg. A week later four pale green eggs lay in the nest and she began to incubate them. Then for nearly a month the two birds took turns on the nest. One fished while the other sat on the eggs, keeping them warm. While one sat, the other fished or hovered nearby.

With her mother sick, Emily became too busy to watch for the bird.

Still, from the corner of her eye, she would have noticed had he flown nearby.

The Wentworth's supply of winter food grew slowly. Emily continued to bring into the house the strange plants and small animals she found. One day it would be a pink rock or a white shell that had been smoothed and rounded by countless tides. The next it might be a wild flower that burst into bloom under the warming sun. She found a stubby, translucent, water-swollen plant that grew in patches over the marsh. She could almost see through the plant's skin to the inside. In wonder she carried it to her mother.

"These are the samphire I told you about. At least that's what they are called back home. Goodness knows what they are called here," Mary said as she held the plant up to the light of the window. "They make good pickles. You might gather more."

Emily brought a basketful of the plants and Mary got up long enough to put them in a large crock with vinegar, sugar, bay leaf, which Emily picked from the shrubs lining the upland, a few peppercorns, and dill tops from the garden. After they had set for a week Emily put them in small crock jars and lined them up on a shelf.

With the warm weather came mosquitoes and sand flies. After a warm rain the mosquitoes swarmed from the brackish little drained marsh pools. The insects grew so unbearable that Elias had to build a smudge fire near the house to keep the noxious pests away. Smoke poured into the house when the errant wind turned. Mary hastily closed the windows. Soon the house became stifling and she was forced to open them again. She struggled all day keeping a balance between climate and pests.

Houseflies buzzed lazily in the summer heat. They alighted here and there, walking over dung, then food, as they flew from neighboring barnyards to the Wentworth's kitchen.

One morning, when steam was already rising from the marsh, Mary awoke with a headache. She cooked a breakfast of porridge but then began to feel dizzy and sank onto her bed. This feeling she did not understand for it was not the consumption that she lived with daily — the disease that ate at her lungs. This was another. Her nose ran. Her throat burned. She developed a fever. She didn't tell Elias, for she thought it might be only catarrh or some such that would soon pass. By the next morning a fever raged through her thin body. She did not get out of bed. Elias abandoned his work for the day and wetted cloths with cold well water to place on her forehead. The burning abated not a whit. He tried rubbing her arms with alcohol to reduce the fever. Mary had a bit of relief but then the fever raged again.

Emily ran out of the house and down to the marsh. Herself anxious, she felt abandoned by everyone. Her father had not even noticed her presence as she hovered near trying to help. She had tried to eat the cold porridge from the pot but the gummy cereal stuck to the roof of her mouth. Her mother, wrapped in delirium, was not aware of anyone. She had turned inward and rambled and muttered and shouted disjointed memories of her childhood.

The marsh was strangely quiet. For some reason this morning no animals were visible. The estuary was empty and glassily still. Emily moved disconsolately about, gathering clams. She prepared a small supper but her father would not eat and her mother could not. For a time Mary was quiet. Emily and Elias dozed before the fire. But not for long.

Mary began to rage irrationally and finally lapsed into deep delirium. She thrashed about and tried repeatedly to get up. Elias was awake all night soothing her and working to reduce the fever. Dawn finally came after the desperate hours. Elias looked worn out. Still he dressed and left the house. Emily was gathering firewood.

"Keep changing the cloths on her head," he said. "And fan her. I'm going for help." He disappeared down the cartway.

Emily felt panic rise in her throat. Her mother lay sick unto death and Emily did not have the least idea how to care for her. What if she were to die before her father returned? What should she do then?

Mary again tried to get out of bed. Desperately Emily

tried to hold her down. When it seemed her mother would overpower her, Elias returned, followed by a woman wearing a lightweight black shawl pulled hard around her shoulders. Her hair, too, was pulled hard back and gathered at the nape of her neck. Although her mouth was set in a grim line, her eyes were kind.

"How do! I'm Mrs. Phillips. Your papa told me your mother was ailing. I've come to see if I can help."

Now that she had support Emily began to cry. She stood over her mother beside Mrs. Phillips and sobs tore through her body. Her mother's face glistened with sweat. Her hair hung lank and wet about her pain-filled face. The blanket covering her was wet.

"She's sick, all right. There's no mistake about that! It's the vapors and fever. You get it when you first come here, and then if you live through it, you are all right from then on." She turned to Elias. "Now you go off to my house and tell Mr. Phillips to take you to fetch Granny Tate!" She turned to Emily and took her arm. "Your pa's gone off to get Granny Tate from Dogtown. She'll know what to do if anyone does."

The fears and anxieties of two days burst forth in a torrent of tears from Elias. Grief etched every line of his face. Emily had never seen her father cry, or any man cry. She in turn wailed utterly disconsolate.

"That don't help!" Mrs. Phillips said. "What we need to do is see she don't hurt herself if she gets the convulsions." Elias's shoulders squared as he tried to gain control of himself. Stumbling, he left to get Mr. Phillips.

"Help me!" the woman commanded. Emily froze. "Fetch me a sheet!" Emily did as she was told and watched in horror as Mrs. Phillips tore it into strips. Mary would rather have died than rip one of her precious linens.

They bound Mary's arms to her sides with long bands of

[86]

sheeting to keep her from hurting herself. Then they wrapped her in the remains of the sheet which Mrs. Phillips wetted with cool water from the bucket. "Fetch another bucketful of water!" she said. Emily quickly ran out of the house, relieved to be out of the sick woman's presence, guilty for the stolen relief.

The sheet seemed to get warm as soon as it was applied. It had been rewetted for the eighth time when they heard hoofbeats in the yard. Elias and Granny Tate climbed down from the beast's back. Emily nearly fainted when she saw the witchy-looking old woman who came through the door. Grizzled hair escaped from beneath a black cloth tied around her head. She had no teeth. One eye was cast wildly while the other looked straight ahead. The fingers of her hands seemed gnarled into lumps and they were caked and cracked. She wore no shoes.

She hobbled over to Mary and took her hand. She looked beneath the woman's eyelids and opened her mouth. The old woman muttered constantly. Then she got up abruptly and took a bundle of herbs from a cloth roll she wore around her waist. While Emily stood tearfully aside with her hand to her mouth, the old woman appropriated the cooking pot, threw the herbs in, poured in some water, and brewed up the concoction, constantly stirring it. Then she unbound Mary, forced her body to a sitting position, pressed her tongue down with the handle of a spoon, and poured some of the steaming liquid down her throat.

"Papa!" Emily said desperately.

"It's all right, girl. It's all right." Elias put his arm around her roughly for a moment, then looked to his ill wife, withdrawing into himself.

"You go home," Granny Tate said to Mrs. Phillips. "You go home now. This will take all night."

"I do have the mister and the children," she said. In

truth there was nothing further she could do. Mrs. Phillips left, the flame of her lantern growing smaller and smaller and finally disappearing from sight.

Granny Tate sat on a stool and watched Mary. Half an hour passed. Once again she poured the brew down her throat. This time Mary began to shake uncontrollably. Again they bound her arms to her sides. Then the old woman sat down to wait. She took out a pipe, stuffed it with another herb, and smoked away until it seemed she was on fire. Some of the smoke she blew into Mary's ears.

When dawn broke over the horizon, Mary's fever broke with it. She fell into a deep sleep. Granny Tate chuckled. "Never fails. Got that receipt from an Injun, and it's a good 'un! What she needs now is to sleep. Don't let her lie too long though. She mus' sit up with pillows behind her."

Emily grabbed the old woman's gnarled hands. "Thank you, thank you!"

"Eh? Thank me? Not yet. Not by half! We're not through with this yet for that woman is grievous ill. I'll just take this ladle now though." She plucked the large wooden ladle that was hanging on the wall and tucked it in the cloth roll at her waist.

Without further words she went toward the horse. Elias helped her up and mounted behind her. "I'll take her back to Dogtown. You watch your mother!" Elias said to Emily.

Emily felt the slow thudding vibration as the horse plodded off with its double burden. Again Emily was alone with Mary. The house seemed very empty and still except for the labored breathing of her mother on the bed.

Emily watched anxiously but Mary slept on. Finally the tired girl began to doze as the warm sun poured in through the window. Suddenly Mary began to cough. She started up like a wild woman. She clutched her chest. Blood began

[88]

to flow from her mouth and nose. Emily jumped to her feet and tried to stop the flow with a piece of sheeting but there was nothing she could do. There was nothing she could do!

In one minute the blood had drenched Mary's nightgown and the coverlet under which she lay. Mary's head fell back on the pillow. She lay very still, her face a mask of agony. Within one more minute she stopped breathing, her eyes open staring at nothing.

Emily screamed in panic as her mother's life ebbed away, then ran out of the house toward the marsh. She threw herself across her special rock, its hard, unyielding surface pressing against her face, and cried piteously. The marsh gave up its morning sounds. Birds flew by unmindful of her sorrow. The water that had been flowing quietly into the marsh had reached that mystical moment when the tide turned. Quietly it reversed itself and began its ebb out to sea.

Finally Emily roused herself. A long way off she glimpsed the great blue heron flying slowly, but he was flying away and not toward her. She felt totally abandoned. With leaden feet she walked back up the hillock toward the house. She knew she must put things right before her father returned.

The sun was straight up at noon as Elias walked into the farm clearing. Emily was washing the bloody sheeting in the tub over which her mother had bent many times. Father looked at daughter, at the tub, at the sheeting, and with a guttural cry ran inside the house.

There was no sound from the death room. Then Elias came out, his eyes wild, his fists clenched. He stalked up to Emily on stiff legs and struck her. She raised her hand to her mouth in pain and surprise. It was as if Elias blamed her for letting Mary die while he was away.

Emily's world collapsed. Where there was color before,

the world was now gray. An internal roar replaced all natural sound. She began to shake and half fell, half sat down on the earth, clutching at it as she had clutched at her mother when she was small.

As quickly as the rage had come to Elias, it left. He turned back and started toward the house, unmindful of Emily. Sensations slowly returned to the girl on the ground. The cree of gulls fighting each other reached her ears. The marsh below her gradually turned from gray to green. Her throat burned from crying. Her hands still shook as she got up and walked back toward the washtub. When the wet bedclothes were finally hung on the fence she forced herself back to the house.

Her father sat by her dead mother and held her hand. All the rest of the day he sat by her. Emily made coffee and handed Elias a steaming cup. He took it absently and set it down on the floor nearby. Again he took his dead wife's hand.

"Papa — Papa!" But Elias did not answer.

Emily crept to her bed. She did not blow the candle out but left it glowing like a vigil light as she fell into a fitful sleep.

She awoke as light streaked the horizon. Her father sat in the same spot with his head bent. Now he no longer held Mary's hand. He seemed, himself, as still as death.

"Papa!" Emily said. "We must dig a grave." Still Elias did not answer. Emily dressed, set her mind to the task, and in the breaking dawn went outside to choose a spot. A warm breeze blew up from across the marsh, and across its wide expanse from the sea. Emily wished the family back across that sea to their home in England, to happy days they had spent in preparation for their move. The knowledge that they could never go back settled on her. She and her father could only go ahead. The price for their passage to America had been too high. It drained her of all energy.

Then she shook off the feeling and picked up the spade which rested beside the fence and broke ground under a broad oak tree on the highest point of their land.

19

Elias lost all interest in the farm. He stopped working. Emily was forced to keep the pot filled by herself. Her father ate the steamed clams she prepared for him. He ate the warm bread she baked as her mother had done, and he drank the morning coffee, but he did so without thinking. Desperately Emily tried to take her mother's place while containing her own sorrow. Sadness overcame her as she searched the marsh for food, or fished the creeks. Her only company during these bleak days were the small birds that flitted among the tall stalks of marsh grass edging the streamsides. Meadow larks flocked over the marsh surface to eat grasshoppers and she searched their nests for eggs. She found where marsh rabbits hid in tunnels under the dense mat of grass. The buzz of crickets surrounded her.

One day a large flock of passenger pigeons flew over the farm. The whir of their wings filled Emily's ears. So densely did they fly that they darkened the sky, their steel-blue and russet-colored bodies blotting out the sun. It must have been an hour before the last bird had disappeared into the tall trees of the deep woods, never to reappear over the farm.

Emily watched daily for the great blue heron. Still he did not come to fish. It was as if he had abandoned his claim to the marsh altogether, a claim that Emily was steadily taking onto herself. In the month since the bird had disappeared the girl had witnessed her mother's death and her father's disintegration from grief. She had grown from a child, fearful and timid, to a whole person, who took solace and strength from the wildness of the marsh and its creatures.

While she gathered strength, the heron remained at the heronry and fed on marsh closer to the nest. Three of the four pale green eggs hatched in one day. The chicks lay in the bottom of the nest exhausted and helpless after the trauma of breaking through the tough eggshells. The mother warmed them under her body while their scraggly, downy feathers dried.

The next day the chick in the fourth egg began to pip. It managed to break a hole in the shell but then could work no longer. It lay still while the other chicks broke the shell in their scrambling for food. Finally the female heron pushed the broken shell and dead chick over the side of the nest.

Both parent birds worked hard to feed their demanding young. All day they fished, alternately and occasionally together, flying from marsh to nest. They fed the chicks partly digested food in the beginning. Then as they grew older the herons deposited whole, small fish in the nest for the young to pick up.

All through the heronry young birds clambered inexpertly over the tree branches. Covered with mouse-gray and olive-gray down they teetered and squawked and squealed. Sometimes a raccoon rummaged about the forest floor and cast its eyes upward to the nest. Some young herons regurgitated half-digested fish toward the interloper. If a bold raccoon climbed a tree despite the adult birds nearby and the height of the nests, the young birds regurgitated until their food was gone. Then they would turn around and jet feces downward. Although few predators stalked the heronry only three-fourths of the chicks lived to grow their juvenile plumage, dark gray crown, white cheeks and throat, gray back, and pinkish-cinnamon breast and thighs.

As the young birds grew, Emily grew, gaining knowledge and hardening her muscles with work. Her face tanned deeply under the summer sun because she went without a bonnet. Her water-ruined boots lay neglected under her bed. She often worked with her skirt hiked up about her waist, her calves and feet bare.

She sat for a time each day on her favorite watching rock and looked over the salt meadow. She learned the comings and the goings of the tides and how high they reached during different phases of the moon. She watched marsh hawks sail back and forth, occasionally disappearing from her sight as they dropped down for a mouse running through the grass. She listened to wrens sing and watched them weave their basket nests among the tall marsh grass stalks. She watched an osprey take fish from the stream, and fly back to its nest, a big platform of sticks atop a disstant, dead tree.

On her way across the marsh she stumbled on a nest of twigs and reeds. Emily would never have known the nest existed if she hadn't frightened a female bittern from her eggs. Carefully Emily parted the grass and saw four greenish-white eggs. The bird had flown only a short distance and called piteously. Emily shrank back and waited for the bird to return but it was wary. She would have robbed an egg or two, but she told herself they were laid too long ago. She left them to hatch and returned to the house, fearful the bittern would abandon the nest altogether if she did not. She felt protective of the small creatures while the monarch of the marsh was absent.

In the late afternoons, after Emily had filled the pot and cooked supper, she watched great numbers of darting, fluttering barn swallows swoop and dart over the marsh, after the clouds of mosquitoes that rose from brackish pools. She never tired of watching the setting sun glinting off the swallows' steel-blue backs.

One night, as the candle guttered in its holder, Emily saw Elias stir. He stood up and poked the dying embers in the fireplace. By the light of a single candle and the fire he unpacked his cobbler's tools. He turned over the hammer and the awl thoughtfully in his hands, then left them overnight on the bench before the hearthstone.

The next day he took two silver teaspoons from the six that had been Mary's only dowry. He walked to Gloucester, sold the spoons and bought a thick, tanned hide. For two days he cut and pegged. Finally from the leather emerged a stout pair of boots.

Granny Tate pronounced them the finest she had ever seen. Elias gave them to her in payment for her vigil over Mary. The old woman showed them off when she walked to High Street to trade herbs for staples. Soon everyone knew that Elias Wentworth cobbled.

As the days passed Elias spent much of his time inside the house over his work. It was as if his taste for farming was held in limbo and that he must relive part of his past with Mary.

His desire for food increased slightly. He ate what was put before him, hardly speaking to the lonely girl who hovered near. When he had accumulated several pairs of shoes he carried them into Gloucester for sale. With some of the money he bought more leather. A few of the clinking coppers he put beneath a loose brick in the fireplace. One day he brought home an old cow, payment for cobbling boots for a family of twelve. The trade which he had put behind him in England now crowded back to him as people came with shoes and boots to be mended.

Emily went at the chores without complaint. She did resent the time she spent tending the garden Elias had started. The soil was unworkable, unsuited to the planting of vegetables, and yielded up a stunted crop. Mary had worked over it, but now the small patch had gone to weeds. Emily managed to divide between present and future eating the few vegetables that did grow.

The girl anxiously looked at the marks Elias had notched on the fence post nearest the house and saw that sixty days since their arrival had come and flown like the wind. Sixty suns had come up, even though some had been shrouded by fog, some blotted out by rain, but sixty precious days had marched by in relentless fashion. Many a night found her so exhausted she fell into bed with most of her clothes on, but she was determined to set store for the winter.

Each day it seemed the burdens on Emily grew ever greater. Daily she now had to bring three armloads of fully grown salt hay for the cow to chew, swallow, and then rechew. Sometimes she led the old cow off by a rope around her horns to the upland and staked her out to eat grass.

Other times she let the beast browse through the woods. In reward the cow gave warm, rich milk.

Emily went to the edges of the woods to pick blueberries from low-growing bushes. Most of the berries she crushed, sprinkled with sugar, and spread out to dry on a flat dish in the sun. But some she put in the kettle, lined with dough, to make a pudding pie.

That night she proudly served the dish, pouring over it a pitcher of cream. Elias ate the pie, made with such love and invention, with no more thought or comment than he gave the beans or corn bread or clams that made up their staple fare.

Disappointment soured Emily's triumph. Her longing for a kind word from her father rose in a bitter lump in her throat. She missed her father's touch and his occasional smile. She mourned her mother's death silently and alone. Her only solace was climbing atop the watching rock at the head of the marsh. From it she scanned the sky for the heron or lay across it looking down into the gently flowing stream.

While she worked and watched from her rock, the young herons in the heronry grew stronger. They now spent most of the time clambering through the treetops. Occasionally an awkward young heron would plunge to his death and quickly be seized by a predator. Other herons, unmindful of the fallen bird, tested their wings. They climbed over each other at the approach of the adult birds who flew in with fish hanging crossways from their strong bills.

Emily's wait for the great blue heron was in vain. She scanned the empty sky and turned her eyes to the marsh grass. She stopped to watch a spider weave her web, crouching over the small animal to get a closer view. Suddenly she felt the shadow of a great bird. For a moment she thought surely it was her heron returned. She quickly looked up and saw, instead, an eagle with fierce yellow eyes. Such an eagle it was! Its wings spread wider than her father was tall.

She felt a rush of wind as the bird flew by. Glistening white feathers capped his head. As he dropped his feet, Emily clearly saw wickedly sharp talons. The bird changed his flight pattern. With braking wing beats he dove out of the sky. Suddenly, with a balled foot, he hit a hidden rabbit in the grass a short distance away. The strike was so hard that the rabbit was thrown three feet into the air. The eagle quickly hopped after the dead animal, its back broken by the blow, and picked it up. Emily watched open-mouthed as the massive bird flew off, the limp, broken rabbit dangling from its talons. She turned back to the spider, her heart beating wildly.

That evening, after the last rays of the sun disappeared, the sky turned a dark, velvet blue. Emily watched as a fox with two kits came warily from the woods and moved down to the streamside. Just what the animals did in the gathering gloom she couldn't tell, but they soon left, their russet coats fading into the shrubbery as they moved back to the trees.

Most of these happenings she kept to herself, for she felt guilt that she had stolen even this small amount of time from her work. She longed to tell her father about the bald eagle and the death of the rabbit, but she did not. He sat long hours bent over the leather across his lap. Often deep into the night Emily heard the tap of his broad-faced cobbler's hammer.

20

The marsh grass had long grown to its full height. Already some of the fine salt hay plants were bending over and carrying others with them. Here and there on the marsh surface the familiar cowlick pattern began to take shape. The summer burst through its peak and set toward fall.

Greenhead flies bothered the cow terribly. She lashed her brush-tipped tail from side to side to rid herself of them but by nightfall her legs often ran with blood. After milking, Emily coated the wounds with lard. She didn't know if this would harm the cow, but at least the flies couldn't bite through the smear and reopen the wounds.

Emily had to stay out of the marsh. Even with her long skirt and her sleeves rolled down the flies bit through and attacked her face and hands. There was no chowder during insect season for she could not go clamming on the rich mud flats. It was three weeks before Emily ventured onto the marsh and into the clam beds. She was bent to her task, unmindful of the marsh or sky beyond, when the great blue heron returned.

Emily glanced up, thinking it might be the bald eagle. A lurch of recognition coursed through her body as she spotted the crooked bill. For a short time she was stunned into inactivity. Then she waved and hallooed to her bird. Her spirits soared.

"I'm angry with you, you know. Off you go without a word. Then back you come without a word. I suppose you'll want your marsh back now, eh?" She said the words readily enough but the thought of handing over her special place gave her a pang of remorse. "We'll share instead!" she found herself saying in surprise, remembering her dread and even fear of the marsh. The heron paid not the slightest attention and began his imperial stalking of meadow mice.

A short time later another great blue heron flew in and settled on the back of the stream, not far from the heron with the crooked bill. Soon three more, not as large and devoid of the long plumes of the adults, settled beside their parents.

Emily looked up in surprise. "So, that's where you've been!" she said. "And got yourself a family too. I should have known that's what your spring dance meant."

The heron family fed and preened then flew off to an open part of the marsh where they dropped and stood grandly. The heron reclaimed his right to the marsh as though he had never been away.

That night, after she had gone to bed, for the first time in weeks Emily cried. Something about the return of the heron had released a floodtide of tears kept dammed since her mother's death. She could not control herself. She wept loud in agony.

Elias, who was working on a pair of shoes in front of a low fire, stopped with his hammer in midair as Emily burst into tears.

The sound of another's crying penetrated Emily's consciousness. An echo of her own sadness came to her as Elias broke down and wept. Finally, her tears spent, Emily fell into a deep sleep. Elias cried on, then too went to the bed he had shared with Mary and slept.

The next morning he got up and busied himself laying the fire. Emily awoke to the smell of coffee brewing and for a moment thought her mother was bending over the fireplace. Then she saw the stooped shoulders of her father and watched in silent wonder as he prepared porridge for their breakfast. Neither of them spoke of the night, but from that morning on Elias began working on the farm again. He cleared more of the upland, cutting, pulling, and burning stumps. He fenced in a pasture and built a three-sided shelter of logs for the cow. He weeded the garden to coax a few more vegetables from it before fall.

Haying season came. Elias followed the lead of his neighbors and took a scythe out onto the salt meadow. For the whole day he plied blade against grass stalks. Great swaths of cut salt hay covered the surface of marsh on the richest site near high ground. He went to the Phillipses' to learn how to stack this new hay, for it would not behave like the upland hay he was used to in his youth. Then too, that had been long years before. He learned how to lay the hay on stakes where it would be above reach of high tides, but still close enough to be gotten in for the cow during the winter. Before stacking it, Elias let the hay dry for a day. The next day proved fair as well. Emily worked beside her father, gathering and carrying the dried hay to the staddles. Her back and arms had grown strong during the summer. And she had grown an inch in height. But the unusual work made both Emily's and Elias's muscles ache. Both were bone tired when they went inside for a supper of cold pease porridge and bread.

That evening, just before sundown, clouds gathered ominously in the southeast. They spread quickly over the landscape with a moving shadow. Then the wind blew. Elias looked anxiously upward as he watered the cow. Emily's dress whipped about her legs as she milked.

During the night the rising wind invaded every crack in the walls. Finally it howled in full fury. Sheets of rain dashed the side of the house and ran in torrents off the thatched roof. The shrieking wind rattled the glass in the windows. The candles, putting forth a small glow in the gloomy interior, guttered out in the draft. So much water ran down the chimney that the fire was nearly extinguished.

When the storm raged at its height Elias dressed and went outside, bending into the wind and rain. Soon he was back, leading the cow. Emily was up trying to keep the fire alight. "The lean-to's gone," Elias said. "The cow can never stand the weather outside. We'll keep her here until the wind dies down. Let's hope the house still stands when this blow is over."

In answer to his words, a tearing sound came from above their heads. A section of roof blew away. Rain poured through the torn thatch in earnest.

"Papa!" Panic grew inside Emily. It was like a storm at sea with the ship foundering.

"Quick, Em! Everything that will spoil goes in your room." They moved the leather he had worked hard to purchase and the cobbler's tools to a spot under Emily's bed. They snatched a few clothes hung on pegs around the room and flung them into her room as well. Then they pushed table and benches into a corner to make a barrier around the cow. Through the rest of the night Elias and Emily huddled together on the bed.

Toward morning the storm dropped suddenly. Quiet settled around them. The sudden drop after the howling intensity left them with an uneasy feeling. Emily cooked hominy grits, talking angrily to the fire as the wet wood sputtered and steamed. Elias took the cow outside and tied her to a tree. Soon he was back in the house.

"Mr. Phillips says this is the eye of the storm passing and we can expect more." Emily's chin dropped in dismay but she set to work and mopped up as much of the water standing on the floor as she could.

During the lull Elias managed to nail boards over the hole in the roof. Emily went to the garden, where ruin met her eyes. The cornstalks were broken. Most of the carrots were washed out of their bed by the deluge. She picked as many as she could and carried them inside the house. Then Elias moved the cow indoors again and the storm duplicated itself.

By afternoon of the following day the last of the rushing clouds passed overhead. Almost in mockery, it seemed, the sun came out. Such a blue sky never was before. The air was wonderfully fresh. Water quickly drained from rocks and off the sandy surface of the upland. Most of the barnyard stood deep in water but Elias put the cow in anyway.

Fallen trees lay about on the upland. Leaves were plastered on tree trunks and rocks. More destruction dotted the marsh surface. The haystack that Elias and Emily had slaved over lay scattered in a wide pattern. Hardly two blades of grass remained together.

The roof was soon repaired. The house was opened up and dried out but some of the floorboards, warped from the dousing, never did recover their former shape. Elias chopped many fallen trees into firewood for the winter. The land renewed itself, but a large area of low marsh closest to the sea had been completely flooded. The high, wind-driven seas had washed the protective dunes away. Now wave after wave inundated the marsh, tearing at the plant cover. Large sections of creek bank slumped into the water and were carried away to the sea. Part of the Wentworths' valuable salt hay meadow existed no more.

Rivulets of rain water still drained from the surface. The uncut grasses lay drenched and flattened. To one side, standing in the stream, were the great blue herons as unconcerned as ever. But now one was missing.

The herons' nest had blown apart in the storm. When he lost his footing during the height of the gale, the weakest of the young birds was cast against a cedar trunk. The passing storm left him a sodden, feathery bundle at the base of the tree.

21

The marsh changed with the passing days. Steadily it lost its fresh green color. Golden-brown hues crept in to cover large areas where the salt hay lay on the surface. More and more often the still figures of the heron family were framed against a backdrop of grass and water.

Lavender asters bloomed here and there. Poison ivy leaves turned from bright shiny green to deep red. Bayberry plants on the upland side of the marsh grayed. As she drew close Emily saw the white berries clustered on branches and twigs. When she picked them she noticed that the white berries bore a covering of wax, which smelled wonderfully fragrant. Cedar waxwings were already visiting the bushes to eat the fruit.

Emily took the berries into the house. They lay on the

table when Mrs. Phillips came on one of her infrequent visits. She had brought Emily a piece of homespun.

"I see you've got yourself some bayberries. They make the best candles in the world!" she said. "All you need is patience, and berries of course, and firewood, lots of it." She gave Emily instructions which sounded simple enough but they masked the great amount of work involved.

For three days Emily gathered berries. For three more days she boiled them in the clothes pot in the yard and skimmed off the wax that rose to the surface. Then she tied weighted wicks from a long stick which she rested over the top of the kettle. She dipped the wicks in the wax. With each dipping a thin coating of the greenish-gray wax was laid down. The wax hardened when the stick was lifted off the pot. After repeated dippings the candles were formed. In the end Emily had nearly a hundred candles, not enough for the whole winter, but augmented with the inferior tallow candles that sputtered, they would last and keep the house fragrant with their scent.

Emily and Elias, used to getting up with the sun and working through the daylight hours, now found their working day much shortened. They ate supper earlier and spent more and more time in front of the fire. Elias used some of the time after supper to work on furniture. He built a table of pine for which he had the legs turned on a foot-powered lathe in Gloucester. He made chairs of oak and rushed the seats with giant papyrus which grew in freshwater ditches on the upland behind the house.

Elias kept cobbling as well. These nights the precious candles disappeared one after another but the boots her father worked on were important. They meant bags of cornmeal and whole wheat flour from the grist mill. They meant squares of salt pork and slabs of bacon to be hung from the rafters near the fireplace.

Barrels of herring and salted marsh birds stood in a far corner of the room. These would see them through the winter. The last turnips and carrots from the garden were packed in sand in a tub and placed by the herring. Parsnips still lay in the ground and would be dug only as needed, even if Elias would have to get them out of the frozen ground with pick and shovel. Hay for the cow was brought up to the barnyard. The old beast still gave some milk but she would soon have to be freshened with a new calf. Elias made inquiry in town as to who owned a bull. They had no chickens, but neighbors gave them eggs in exchange for a sole on a pair of boots or a bit of harness mending.

Fewer and fewer animals were on the marsh now. Many of the birds had already migrated to winter feeding grounds. Raccoons, the young now almost indistinguishable from the parents, all looking very round with stored fat, still fished the streamsides, but they too would soon disappear to a den in a hollow tree. Elias shot two of the young ones and with the skins, which he scraped and tanned, made himself and Emily warm hats to cover their ears through the coming winter.

The older great blue herons sat with heads pulled low. The young fished and caught mice from the hay meadow, still building strength into their muscles.

Then one mellow fall day Elias decided to go to Gloucester to sell the boots he had made and lined up under his bench. For a trip like this he would borrow the Phillipses' horse and wagon. He went off whistling to the neighbors, then returned to pick up the boots. Emily heard the clatter of wheels on stone and ran out of doors. She looked pleadingly up at her father.

"Well, you want to come with me?"

"Oh, Papa! Could I?"

"You'll need your bonnet and why don't you wear those

new boots you'll find under your bed. Good advertising as it were."

Emily ran into the house and scrambled for the boots. Quickly she put them on with trembling fingers. She looked down at them in admiration. Such beautiful boots she had never seen and they were hers! Elias had made them of soft kidskin, dyed blue. The wonderful boots had scallops running down the sides and a black button nestled in each scallop. It had been so long that she had gone like a wild thing over the marsh and upland that she had almost forgotten about wearing shoes. She felt a small pang as she pulled the boots on for she hated giving up even this small amount of freedom. But the lure of Gloucester overcame her momentary reluctance.

Quickly she threw off her apron and donned her cap. Elias still waited, impatient now to get moving. Emily ran out to him.

All the way to Gloucester Emily's eyes devoured the landscape she had seen only once before. She was a very different girl from the wan, skinny creature who had ridden in the back of the two-wheeled cart their first day off the boat. She had changed from town girl to country lass. Her young muscles had toughened under the hard work of farm living. Her sun-browned skin glowed with health.

Her eyes sparkled as she looked at the craggy rocks sticking up through the soil beside the road. She looked off into the forests and counted the trees that had fallen during the big storm. She watched the birds circling the sky. For a dark moment she thought of her mother. The moment passed and she went back to looking at the countryside. She loved every creature, rock, and tree she saw.

Most of all Emily loved watching the people who worked around their houses or walked or rode on the dirt highway to town. The people raised their hands to their caps in a small salute. Not all were friendly, but most smiled an answer when Elias called a greeting.

Emily's eyes gleamed with excitement as they approached the main shopping area on High Street. All of the wonder of seeing Gloucester for the first time came flooding back. She looked down the hill toward the harbor and saw the masts of many ships. The same noises that had struck her ear that first day came to her from a distance. She heard the rumble of drays moving between ships and warehouses. She heard the laughter of people from taverns and inns. The population may have been only a few thousand, but to Emily, who had spent the whole summer with only her family and a few neighbors, it seemed as if every person in the world was out on this day.

Elias had brought his tools and set up a makeshift shop in the back of his wagon. A small crowd gathered around him and gladly stood in bare feet or thick, coarse stockings while he mended their shoes. He carefully tucked the money he received in a pouch and put it in his inside pocket.

Some of the people stopped to chat and talk politics. She couldn't follow the conversation but Emily knew from the way they smiled at her father that they liked what he said. She looked at her father proudly. He seemed tall and wonderful. She hadn't realized he was a man who could command such looks from people.

The sun hung low when Elias packed up his tools. They would still have time to buy supplies before starting home. Elias stopped the wagon in front of a grocer's who displayed apples, crackers, and potatoes in barrels. A great wheel of cheese rested on a marble slab. Elias bought a large wedge and took a bite of it. Then he gave a chunk to Emily. The mellow cheese warmed her stomach and she realized she was ravenously hungry. As an added treat Elias bought her a piece of horehound candy, big enough to last all the way home.

Darkness was stealing over the land as they drove wearily into the yard. Emily got down and went inside while Elias returned the horse and wagon with a pound of coffee for the Phillipses' kindness.

22

As the first glow of dawn broke over the horizon, Emily awoke to a cold breeze blowing through her window. She dressed, slipped to the fireplace, and took a piece of bread from the brick oven beside the hearth. Elias still slept.

Emily walked down the hill to her rock. This was the best time of day on the marsh. Small noises traveled to her through the clear air. Fish splashed in the creeks. Birds called to each other in the lightening day. She saw herself as only a small figure in a large landscape.

"What has happened to me?" she wondered. No longer did she fear the world, the wild creatures that roamed the marsh, the strange, pungent smell of decaying and growing vegetation. A peace settled over her.

Out of the rose fingers of the sun flew the pair of great

blue herons followed by the two young birds. Unmindful of her they settled in the winding creek. They stood very still, silhouetted against the sky. A sense of the timelessness of their existence came over Emily. She had trespassed their world and shared their ways, gathering what the family needed. She wished for some sort of sign that they recognized her, but the herons stood motionless, reflected in the water.

When Emily left the rock to attend to her chores they did not move. She fed and drew water for the cow. Then she split firewood, laid a fire, and made griddle cakes. Elias got up yawning, ate breakfast, and set about his work.

The day passed slowly. Several times Emily stopped her chores to look out over the marsh. The herons still stood as they had during the morning. An autumn breeze stirred her skirt and blew her hair about her face. Late in the afternoon she again walked to her watching rock. Now the herons seemed restless. They shifted position and turned into the wind.

The wind picked up, blowing from the north. Emily shivered as the chill played over her bare arms.

The great blue heron lifted his head and pointed his crooked bill skyward. He shook his body and with some preliminary flexing of his wings, lifted himself up into the air with slow, powerful wing beats. Immediately the other herons followed. With her special heron in the lead, they turned directly south and began the autumn passage.